The Understanding

A NOVEL

Jane Barker Wright

The Porcupine's Quill

NATIONAL LIBRARY OF CANADA CATALOGUING IN PUBLICATION DATA

Wright, Jane Barker, 1953–
The understanding / Jane Barker Wright.

ISBN 0-88984-242-6

I. Title.

PS8595.R5915U5 2002   C813'.54   C2002-903188-5
PR9199.3W67U5 2002

1 2 3 4 • 04 03 02

Published by The Porcupine's Quill,
68 Main Street, Erin, Ontario N0B 1T0.
www.sentex.net/~pql

Represented in Canada by the Literary Press Group.
Trade orders are available from University of Toronto Press.

We acknowledge the support of the Ontario Arts Council,
and the Canada Council for the Arts for our publishing program.
The financial support of the Government of Canada
through the Book Publishing Industry Development Program
is also gratefully acknowledged.

Canadä

The Canada Council | Le Conseil des Arts
for the Arts | du Canada

ONTARIO ARTS COUNCIL
CONSEIL DES ARTS DE L'ONTARIO

For Nick and Henry,
without whom this book
would have been written much faster

Chapter One

Friday night you go to Solly and Isobel's. You make something or buy something and bring that. It doesn't matter what – people bring everything from Cheezies to roast goose – it's the bringing that counts. Isobel still believes in the communal thing, and, God knows, they have enough mouths of their own to feed. They live on rice, mostly. Or so you've been told.

You don't actually have to know them. Their real friends, the ones who come on nights other than Friday, have become middle-aged and cautionary about this: they prophesy concealed weapons, a casing of the joint, a home invasion. They say the world is not what it was. But Solly and Isobel resist this trend against trust and refuse to close the house on Fridays. They've always nursed a childish resentment of sensible advice and they continue to believe that the world is good.

You might be a friend of Solly's, or even a patron (in which case, you're more than welcome – they're not as unworldly as they seem.) You might be another mother and a friend of Isobel's. You might be one of the Project students, his lover, sibling, friend, even his parent. You might be the furnace repairman again, looking for a cheque. You might be a fan of Magnolia White, a daughter of this very house. You might just want to say you'd been there.

It's important that you know the rules. You bring something. You don't become abusive, even to the one you love. You arrive after seven. (Isobel likes to have the little ones in pyjamas before anyone gets there. At the party, they'll become overtired and silly and will fall asleep late, maybe on your lap. If you're wise, you'll avoid them but if you're a woman and after Solly, you'll track them down and try to charm them and they'll stare at you slit-eyed and laugh before darting away like minnows.)

The Whitechapels are the best kind of famous. Solly's name is a byword in certain moneyed international circles; the claim of his acquaintance carries some prestige. And he and Isobel have an appealing eccentricity. They're committed to lost causes; they're uncaring of public opinion. They're the kind of people we all intended to be before we learned to give a shit. Someone once said of them that they got old before they grew up.

This Friday happens in the mid-nineties in Vancouver early in the rainy season, a time and place when everyone is down with flu or despair and the air is so wet you can almost drink it.

Pat Klassen darts past the clump of reporters on the sidewalk and sloshes around to the back of the house where, in the tiny sun porch, three large hooks are already overloaded with soggy coats, each lining sopping up the wet from the coat underneath it so that by the end of the night all the coats, though dry outside, will be lined with a chill pad of damp. Isobel says that her only remaining dream is to build a mudroom. She was never a romantic woman.

Pat is not surprised to find a girl cowering among the coats. There's always a tearful girl on a Friday, just as there's always a drunkenly amorous man. Summer is easier on heartbroken girls. They can hide behind hedges and trees. They can have hysterics in the studio. They can storm off without ruining the effect by searching for adequate footwear.

Pat removes her shiny black cape, hangs it up and steps out of her rubber boots, glancing up at the girl's face as she does so. There's a danger she's a friend of her daughter's. To her relief, she doesn't recognize her. Though kind to her friends, Pat's stingy with sympathy for strangers, whether they're victims of foreign famine or sad girls on sun porches. She believes that suffering is an inevitable part of life and that there's no reason to be gloomy about it. She defines all suffering by her own shallow dip in it.

The kitchen is full of people, noise and steamy, nervous party heat. Pat recognizes with dread the Neighbourhood in the form of a local couple. (When capitalized, the Neighbourhood has nannies and jeeps and condos at Whistler.) The two stand protectively close to each other, not drinking but holding their drinks in front of their faces, scanning the crowd. They look as if they've come straight from vital and impressive work – both are dressed in navy blue suits and fabulous shoes that won't stand for this kind of weather. They'll have heard about the divorce. Even kind people say the wrong thing and make her cry and then cry more, out of anger, because she isn't sad at all, she truly isn't.

They haven't seen her yet and Pat hopes to avoid them. Isobel won't have invited them; she has surprisingly high standards of parents. She and the Neighbourhood assume that this pair have children only because they happened to glance at the clock before it was too late and that children are an experience like Nepal or river-rafting, something not to be missed if you can help it. These children are troublesome and sad and a hazard to local pets. The Neighbourhood considers itself lucky that their days are so encumbered with team sports and improving lessons that they are rarely seen except as fierce little heads in the back of a Suburban driven by a harassed Filipina nanny.

The woman catches Pat's eye just as she tries to deke around her.

'Don't forget the tree meeting!' she calls. What's her name? Shelley, Sherry, Sandy – something like that.

Big old trees are being cut down to improve the view of downtown, the flat blue of English Bay and the abrupt, obscuring thrust of the North Shore mountains. The Neighbourhood doesn't approve.

'The tree thing. I won't,' she promises as she slips into the dining room. She finds she's become ambivalent about trees. She's moved close enough to the edge of the Neighbourhood to feel contempt for its centre.

She picks up some name-brand water: Pat is well-preserved and intends to become more so.

'Seen Isobel?' It's the woman from the *Sun*, in her basic black. How dare she say 'seen Isobel' like that, as if she knows her.

'Seen Solly?' She doesn't ask 'seen Magnolia?' but Magnolia's who she's after. Everyone wants to see the incredible, snarling, sexy, sad Magnolia White, to say they heard her sing 'O Holy Night' at the Christmas concert in 1985, to claim to have foreseen her extraordinary success. Not a suitable name for a girl of her colouring, Pat feels. Peachy Keen would have been better.

'Seen Solly?' the woman asks again, a little desperately.

'Nope,' Pat says with some pride. A few years ago, she'd have been looking for him too or, for a week, he'd have been looking for her: Solly's infatuations have the fleeting glare of a searchlight. Ordinarily a spell of Solly's adoration leaves a woman feeling better rather than worse. His former women are ruefully amused. There's a sense of having joined a club, of holding insider information, of performing a secret ritual in the strictly enforced discretion after the affair. His former women mutter that he's a bastard, and sigh and chuckle and shake their heads, feeling suddenly wise and desirable.

Pat felt wise and guilty and somehow stronger, as if she'd endured a catastrophic event after which mere survival was an achievement. She lost ten pounds, called a divorce lawyer, stopped dyeing her hair, bought a cape and made a friend of Isobel.

The house stinks of cigarettes. There's a sign taped to the front door, which reads 'Welcome to Our Smoke-Filled Home'. The kids put it up hoping to cause shame and repentance but Solly and Isobel smoke anyway and, being smokers, draw smokers from miles away. It's an exponential phenomenon. Health-conscious people think of all those children and shake their heads. Pat can see people doing that now, waving their hands in front of them as they talk. She's doing it herself. If you want Solly and Isobel, you have to take the smoke too. This is what living dangerously has come to in the Neighbourhood.

The hungry young are present, as always. They will be Solly's students and friends of students, here for the free food and booze; here for temporary shelter from the weather. Pat can't afford to be entirely cynical about the Project. Her daughter, Megan, is one of Solly's students and she's worried less about Megan this year than ever before. She watches as the kid who helps Isobel around the house, a phlegmatic girl with a nose-ring, stony as a bouncer, gathers up dirty plates. The Neighbourhood fears they'll be murdered in their beds with all these street kids around, but they don't complain aloud. Solly and Isobel are fashionable these days. So the middle-aged folk, uniformly well fed and well exercised, stand back from the food and sip their drinks and wave their hands gently in front of their noses and study the murals with respectful attention or scan the crowd for acquaintance and celebrity.

Pat recognizes a smooth, malleable, over-large actor's face. She's met him here before. He went to school with Solly, some fancy Toronto school with a name they tend to drop. He was in an American TV series some years back and was briefly famous. Now, people tend to avert their eyes once they recognize him as if his lapse from fame reflects some embarrassing personal flaw. He sees her and grins and she recalls his flair for gossip. She grins back, sits down beside him and waits for Isobel.

'New York, of course,' Bill is saying breezily, as if he owns the place. 'Well, New York's always been online.' When has Bill begun to talk like this? He's always been such a proper and pedantic man; it's the contrast to Solly that makes the relationship work.

The retrospective was Bill's idea. He pitched it to Solly in June when both the property tax and the insurance payment were due. As Solly's agent and business manager, Bill never mentions money; he talks about art. It's Solly who talks about money these days. The Whitechapels have to save up for June and Christmas every year, and every year as their expenses increase, Solly's a little less comfortable with this. June and Christmas arrive so frequently. He would like, just once, to take everyone out to dinner. He would like not to worry about the rattle in the van or the gap between Suzannah's front teeth. Last June, the idea of a large retrospective show, the critical interest, the publicity, the sales, seemed an almost miraculous gift.

'And Liz says L.A.'s a go. Well, you've always sold well there. And retros are great for business in L.A. They do so like to have their taste confirmed down there.' Bill's a very tall man and, because they're in the basement hallway and there's some kind of vent above his head, he has to maintain a painful stoop, but here, at least, he has Solly contained and listening. He's too smooth to blurt out Magnolia's name. He knows Solly too well. But the huge interest in Magnolia can't hurt. They have to use it while it lasts. Bill knows it's too big to last long.

'Most of the collectors have responded. Well, they would, wouldn't they? Their pieces can only increase in value. That's what a retrospective show's all about.'

Bill's feeling uneasy. He's brokered Solly's furniture for years. Selling is something he understands. He knows when to push, when to step back; he knows how at bone level and he'd thought he'd already sold Solly on this. Solly loved the idea in June. He talked about turning the Project into a business, finding factory space in Richmond. There was a light in his eyes. Now in this dim, cramped corridor, Solly blinks like a bear only recently out of hibernation.

'Right,' Solly says, thinking of all those years when Bill was a lifeline, all the pieces sold, one by painstaking one, to pay for shoes and potatoes and school supplies; all those bits of him that are out there, about to increase in value to the benefit of strangers. All he has left are a few prototypes which Isobel saved for household use. They live with rough drafts, experiments gone wrong, stupid ideas. Hot mugs and cigarettes have scarred them. They've been nicked and chipped by the children in their thoughtless violent play. Some are left outside year round, warped and grey and splintering. People put their feet up on them, or scratch them with toy cars and Lego. Yet if they'd been treated like triumphs instead of mistakes, put away and venerated and barely lived with at all, they'd be worth, what, a university degree? An RRSP?

To recognize Solly's name is to admit to membership in that sliver of society which buys furniture with signatures instead of brand names. *That's a Whitechapel*, people will say in defence of an odd looking occasional table in the corner, *there are three in the MOMA*. There will be public eulogies at his death; the value of his pieces will triple and collectors will sigh sadly and grin. It's precisely the kind of fame that suits him. Solly enjoys being fawned over by the few.

Magnolia's fame terrifies him. There's hysteria in it, unruliness, danger. Magnolia's fame has turned a hard white light on his life, which for so long has been lived in flattering amber.

And the Project is going sour just like the Farm did, although not so dramatically but at a staid, middle-aged pace, more like over-cellared wine than milk left out in the heat. When the farm went sour, he ran away and began again. Walking away is different.

No one noticed when Solly Whitechapel began to change. In a fraught and frenetic life, he's established such a complex milieu that lately he's begun to feel like a spider trapped in a huge and intricate web of its own making, a web that has become more important than the spider itself. But then, the spider is never shown its web as if it is his lifelong accomplishment. No one tells the spider to stop spinning, that the web is complete and entire and must now be left alone. The spider doesn't feel trapped by his web or seek methods of dismantling it. The spider simply dies or moves on and lets time and the forces of nature do it for him.

He remembers himself and looks swiftly up at Bill.

'If I start the kids on making reproductions, how much can we expect to clear?' he asks, wondering how he will ever explain this to Isobel.

'Take everything out of that bag,' Isobel is saying, 'and put it right into the wash.'

'Everything?' Pierre asks, holding up a flashlight.

'Don't be a smartass. You know what I mean.' She makes his bed. The basement bedroom, which Pierre shares with Ash, reeks of young men and their preoccupations. Breathing is an invasion of privacy. She opens the tiny window and lets in the clatter the rain makes on the cement sidewalk just outside.

'I mean it. In the washing machine. And sort it. And put in detergent. And turn the big knob halfway to the right. And pull it out. And close the lid.'

Pierre rolls his eyes. People at camp hadn't nagged. 'I know how to run the washer, Mum.'

She raises her eyebrows. 'I may fall over.'

He decides they've bantered enough. As one child among nine, Pierre has learned to make the most of a parent's attention when he's got it. 'So. Mum. You know about the Japanese current, right?'

'Kind of. Don't ball those socks up. They'll never dry.' She's pulling damp, crumpled clothing out of his hockey bag.

'So, the Japanese current is this huge, huge mystery, right? They still don't know its exact path. Amazing, huh? Anyway, they're trying to track it, so you know what they do? They wait, see. And luckily – well, not lucky for everybody but you know what I mean – luckily, every so often a big container ship sinks in the middle of the Pacific, right? And, so people know, well, some people know what's in those containers, right? And the containers break open sometimes, okay? So they tell all the beachcombers all up and down the coast to look out for skis or bath toys or whatever, and call it in if they find any. Give the location and time and stuff, and then they can map the current. So like last year this Japanese ship went over and you know what they were carrying? Nike shoes! You know, the real expensive kind the kids at school wear? Millions and millions of them. So there we were, walking up and down this beach finding hundreds and hundreds of Nike shoes. Jordy even found a matching pair. Size 10, though. Unbelievable, right?'

'Amazing. Were you warm enough, honey?'

'Warm enough?' Outraged, he feels the need to repeat this: 'Warm enough? Shit, Mum, I was tracking the Japanese current out there! I was on the two-way to the Coast Guard! Warm enough! I'm talking valuable scientific research here … not to mention millions of dollars' worth of footwear.' She favours him with her mild, encouraging maternal smile. He gives up. 'Shit, where's Dad?'

She laughs and curls up on the bed. He's right. Solly's better at the idealistic stuff. 'Sure, honey. Go and tell Dad. Last seen being cornered by Bill. There's plenty to eat in the dining room, but laundry first, okay?' She closes her eyes. She isn't sure she'll be able to summon the strength of will and social obligation to get up.

'You okay, Mum?' he asks. She's annoying at times, but he doesn't like to see her lying down like that.

'Fine, just sleepy. Friday,' she says. 'I'll get up in a minute.' She always gets sleepy when she's pregnant.

Frances, Isobel's mother, lights another cigarette and has a good long coughing fit – Vancouver damp always clogs her chest. She has an Easterner's contempt for the West Coast, its feeble weather and the belligerent mellowness of its inhabitants. And, look at her, she's surrounded by these people! Invigorated by resentment, she begins to feel a little better.

Her feet are throbbing inside her sensible shoes. She'll have to sit down soon. She looks around and selects a pale and defenceless boy at whom she directs an enraged elderly glare which causes him to leap up immediately as if charged with electrical current.

'I'm sorry. Excuse me. Would you like to sit down?' he babbles, his shaven head as vulnerable as a baby's – who said skinheads were threatening? A nice polite Canadian boy. She thanks him regally and sits.

Someone shouts 'Gram!' and she spots Ash charging through the crowd towing a petulant-looking girl. 'Mum said you were coming in today. How was your flight? This is Tara.' He presents the girl proudly as if he's made her himself in pottery class. Tara's a tiny little thing but she looks tough enough to snap Ash in two.

'Just this minute. Straight from the airport. You know me. I never stop. Get me a drink, will you, sweetie? Something long and cold. No booze. My throat is parched from that airplane air.'

'Stay here,' he orders Tara, 'I'll be right back.' He lopes off.

Tara stands with her weight on one foot and picks at a scab on her forearm. Frances waits. She speaks for a living and prefers not to squander her voice on mere conversation.

'So,' Tara says finally. 'I hear you're like a really major feminist.'

'Fairly major. In this country anyway.'

'Gloria Steinem's the only one I know. Of course she's so photogenic; you see her a lot.' Here she blushes, a surprising show of sensitivity; Frances is not photogenic. 'Anyway, Ash told me all about you. You should hear him. He goes on and on. But to me, all that political stuff, it's like social studies, right?'

'Right,' Frances agrees, delighted. This rude and ignorant little girl to whom, it seems, she's a colleague of Mrs Pankhurst, has proved her purpose. She's been such a success as to render herself obsolete. She begins to wonder how she can work the anecdote into her speech.

* * *

Willow Whitechapel has always known exactly how beautiful she is. Tonight, she's breathtaking, awe-inspiring, slightly inhuman and scary.

It's the older people who stare and step back. Her contemporaries might stare, but they're careful to sneer too. The young at her parents' parties tend to think beauty is a frivolous idea when applied to anything but art. Willow knows better.

She shrinks slightly into Stephen as they make their progress. The muscles in his forearm swell in proud response.

'I've been in love with you since I was twelve,' she told him, once she picked him out and picked him up, disentangled him from his wife, found an apartment, once they'd acquired sheets and spatulas and toilet brushes. 'You don't remember, do you? Softball?'

This was not a subject about which Stephen was entirely comfortable.

'Sure I remember,' he finally admitted. 'You were the all-intellect one. Not a speck of natural talent and you threw like a girl, but you had the strategy down pat. That was my last year of coaching. You girls were getting so big. You made me nervous. Guess I was right.'

He said it as lightly as he could. He didn't like to hear Willow use a word as resonant as love. Who was to say that abandoning women could not become a habit? They all grew older. So would Willow. Youth, he feared, might be an addiction. His affection for Willow, when analysed, broke down into a blend of avuncular sentiment and sexual thrall. He could smell her youth behind her ears and knees. He loved her hard, childish resilience. He knew the path of love: that its dark, alluring entry, its sudden dips and breathless scrambles would level out eventually and broaden into a smooth, open track. Fresher, rougher trails would beckon and a man who had left the main route once was likely to do so again.

His daughter, Jenny, once Willow's little teammate, had

screamed at him, 'Will's way too old for you, Dad!'

Willow's parents are more or less his age, of course. The father's an oddball, always has been – a great artist, some say. A poseur, say others. Stephen's field is money; he doesn't feel qualified to have an opinion about art. Its market value is different. He owns one of Solly's tables. The purchase of it gave him a small creative thrill. Not many investors are as catholic as Stephen.

Willow's mother, Isobel, breaks his soft heart. It's almost painful to see mother and daughter together, the second so clearly a flashback of the first, sharper and softer at the same time. Other women say she looks her age. As does Willow. Does Willow ever look at her mother and see her future self? He thinks so. At twenty-three, she's already developed the kind of self-discipline that pays off at forty. She's strict about hours of sleep, she neither smokes nor drinks; she takes as much care over creams and lotions as his wife had.

'You'll be pluperfect soon,' he said once.

'Better than subjunctive,' she snapped back, quick as a flash.

Now one of her sisters appears – he's still getting all the siblings straight. Nine children; no wonder Isobel looks tired. This one is still in her school uniform – he remembers Jenny in hers; but Jenny would have died rather wear that tartan outside of school hours.

'Seen Magnolia?' she asks Willow.

'Say hello to Stephen, at least, Winnie. Honestly.'

'Hello, Stephen.'

'Hi there, Winnie. I remember my Jenny wearing that same uniform,' he says.

'You like to look at young girls in school uniform?'

Willow clicks her tongue. 'You know who you sound like, don't you? I mean it. And no, I haven't seen her. I just read the papers like everybody else.' Her eyes pin Winnie like a butterfly.

Winnie's eyes drop. 'She got in yesterday, but she's staying downtown and we don't know if she'll even get over here. There were photographers parked outside all day yesterday, flashing. It was disgusting. If you do see her, send her to Mum. You know how she gets about Maggie. Nice to see you, Stephen. Sorry I'm not wearing my ankle socks.'

Stephen laughs. Winnie, disappointed, stalks off.

'Sorry. These children. Mick'll be practising wrestling holds on you any minute. I do want you to meet my grandmother, though. She's coming in tonight.' Willow flicks a strand of blonde hair over her shoulder. 'Let's get you a drink. I want to show you the house. It'll amuse you.' And she leads him with cool myopic self-containment into the dining room. You'd never know how viciously she pokes at the splinter of her mother's obsession with Magnolia; that she, who is expected to be perfect, gets no credit for being so, as if her perfection were innate and effortless, while Maggie, the problem child, has to be attended, approved, reproved and supervised. It's been there for years. It should be calloused over by now. It shouldn't hurt any more.

'Ah, a mural. Very fashionable,' Stephen remarks.

'That was my Auntie Win. She was Winifred Whitechapel, you know. And it was the opposite of fashionable twenty years ago. Apparently, adornment for its own sake was considered pretentious in those days. Art was supposed to make a political statement.'

Stephen considers this. 'I guess it was.' He hadn't noticed particularly. He'd been busy.

'You can see over there where she's put us in. That's my parents. Me. Ash and Magnolia. The others weren't born of course.'

'But your mother's pregnant. She looks like she's about to deliver forth an army.'

She laughs. 'But that's true, isn't it? Isobel is always pregnant. Maybe that's the political statement. Pregnancy as weaponry. So the mural is redeemed from its despicable beauty.'

Stephen smiles and gently lifts her face so he can admire it. 'The beautiful is as useful as the useful, perhaps more so,' he quotes.

'My God, Stephen, who said that?'

'Victor Hugo.'

'Oh, well, the French,' she says dismissively, 'what can you expect? Besides, I am useful.' She's nettled now. 'I'm very useful. Ask anybody.'

Where are the children? A head count: Monty and Toby have made a nest of blankets under the dining-room table and are assaulting people's feet as they try to get at the food. A soft-hearted student is slipping them crackers. They'll be whining for a drink any minute now. Ash has brought his flinty little girlfriend. Willow's here. Men's heads have turned. Their eyes have softened. They've stopped slouching and have said something to make their partners laugh as Willow glides by on Stephen's arm.

Isobel checks on Suzannah and her friend Margot who are watching *Gone with the Wind* in the basement and salting their popcorn with sentimental tears. Winnie's hiding somewhere being miserable to her diary. Mick's sleeping at a friend's house and, with any luck, Pierre's doing his laundry.

Magnolia could be anywhere. At her hotel, at the 7 Eleven, hiding out or striding out into the pouring rain. The cameras have been outside since yesterday. It's like living under strobe lights. No wonder they call it shooting. Reporters shout questions at her on her way to the Safeway, invade the high school, call the house. They're insatiable. They will poke and probe until everything about Magnolia White is known, or until they lose interest. They'll perform a living autopsy. Maggie's life, everyone's life, will be dissected and exposed because people need some undemanding diversion while waiting for the dentist, the hairdresser, the arrival at the airport, while wasting time.

Magnolia has achieved the wrong kind of fame. What do you want to be when you grow up, people would ask her as people do a child of six or eight or ten. 'Famous,' she would say. It was what she always said. And they would laugh. Famous indeed! How precocious, how cute. And now she *is* famous, anointed by the cover of *People*, referred to nightly on trash TV (looking sweet, surly, demure, depraved, eyes closed, mouth open – it's no wonder that the faces of fashion models lack animation; an ordinary face, when caught mid-expression, can so easily look stupid.) There is Maggie, always different, never quite blending into the background of the family. A cuckoo.

They'll go to the concert tomorrow. They'll have to. She'll watch Magnolia up there, a tiny figure at centre stage picked out by a spotlight like a dust mote caught by a ray of sun. Her child, a part of her, now public property, and how careless the public is of its property.

Isobel chooses not to think about it. She laughs instead at someone's joke and joins the party.

Chapter Two

'I'm stuck here. I told you that. I can't get all the way over there. You're going to have to come to me.'

So they go in shifts like supplicants which leaves Isobel more than a little vexed once she picks up Frances, parks the embarrassing van and sneaks them all into Maggie's preposterous hotel. She can't believe that anyone is this important, least of all a child of hers.

A sleek, hard-eyed assistant allows them into the suite and presents them to Magnolia who's wearing flannelette pyjamas at three in the afternoon, whose hair is unwashed and whose apricot skin is sallow with indolence and recycled air.

The little boys fling themselves at her like wishing pennies, crying *Maggie Maggie Maggie!* They haven't seen her in six months. She clutches them greedily, eyes closed in brief bliss until they begin to squirm and tug at her and demand to be taken on a tour of this magic place with its basket of chocolates there for the eating and the amazing bathroom with tiny wrapped soaps and little bottles of potion.

'What's this for?' Toby asks.

'Let me see. Oh, it's a special cloth for polishing shoes.'

Toby is flabbergasted. 'They make shoes you have to polish? Like wood?'

'Yup. Amazing, eh?'

Soon they're settled a foot away from a huge TV eating chocolates as quickly as they can, with soap in their pockets and the scent of Pan Pacific moisturizer wafting from their hot little bodies.

Frances, unfazed, has poured herself a cup of coffee.

'My darling Magnolia, you look like a sad old tart. Cheer up for once in your life.'

Magnolia grins. 'Misery sells, Gram. It sells big time. I can't afford to be happy.'

'But you're not miserable, are you?'

'Are you kidding? This is like amazing! I get up on that stage. People scream. They like me. They think I have something to say.'

'Then write about that. I, for one, could do with less whining.'

'Gram, you'll ruin me.'

Frances, who is only the grandmother, who has never enforced a curfew for this child, or sent her to her room, or insisted that she eat her beans, can afford to be forthright, while Isobel is doomed to say the wrong thing.

'Honey, are you getting enough sleep? You've got terrible circles under your eyes.'

'Thanks, Mum. I'm working, you know? Touring is hard work. Not just the show, but setups and sound checks. A show every night and the comedown after. You can't go to sleep right away, you know. And the next day you have to fly somewhere else. Like Omaha or something tomorrow. I can't even keep track. This is work. Serious work. It's not like a party or anything.'

It just looks like one. The littered suite smells of smoke and stale booze. Maggie lives in places like this these days, places where the chairs only look comfortable, where there are no reading lamps, where the mound of fruit in the basket tastes of cardboard and wax. Magnolia's belongings don't belong. Her grubby pink teddy, which has been dying of love for years, looks sordid and perverse against a glazed chintz duvet. There are sticky socks in corners and crumpled wet towels on the carpet; miserly ashtrays overflow; people have been here, all right, but it hasn't belonged to any of them.

'But honey, you look so pale and thin. That's not like you.' (Round and plump and pleasing, a golden girl; this is how Magnolia should look, like her mother.)

'Yeah, well, when the tour's over, I'm taking a place in Turkey I heard about. Maybe for me and Ash. Where *is* that guy, anyway? He hasn't been. He's mad, isn't he? I can feel him sulking all the way across town.'

'Oh, honey, he's just busy. He's making an animated film, you know.'

Ash is furious. He refuses to see Magnolia. 'She'll only get a song out of it,' he said. *Twinsy Twinsy* went platinum last spring.

'Little Ashie still at home. You'll never get rid of him, you know.'

'That's not fair. Do you know what rents are here? He's still in school, you know.'

'Oh, yes. Ash is still in school. It's what he does best, being in school.'

And what Magnolia did worst – but look – she's a success now, an amazing success.

'You used to look after one another.' In the schoolyard, first day of kindergarten: Magnolia, pretty and plump, full of smiles – the other mothers tilt their heads and say aww – and Ash paper-white with fear. 'Don't worry, Mum. I'll look after him.' And they walk off toward the big building, holding hands, growing smaller and smaller.

She juggled the two of them, arms aching, never quite attaining the proper arrangement of pillows before she had to answer the demands of their little fishy mouths. There they squirmed, feet entwined, Magnolia the beauty contest baby and blotchy Ash, tugging like lambs at her breasts. A lamb and a doe: gentle creatures. Whatever they recalled of the womb they forgot in the common need for milk, the necessity to curl around each other, to fill each other's gaps. Fed and changed and bathed together, jammed together and jolted along the farm road in Nancy's old carriage among huckleberries and bouquets of alder cones and brodeias, whatever gleanings caught small Willow's eager eye. Thumbs poked into each other's mouths. Food spat out and shared. Later, elaborate schemes for self-destruction: how to climb out of the high chair, teeter at the top of the stairs, reach the electrical outlet. Natter, natter, natter, a language all their own, rich in comment and inflection. Licking dirty tears off each other's faces, screaming over the other's ear infection. Isobel had adored it.

Now this former baby of hers trades wisely on invented misery and looks worn out and her twin won't speak to her, not even in English.

Chapter Three

Toby, the second youngest of Isobel and Solly's children, has crept into their bed at some dark time and has been wriggling and giving voice to the stream of his consciousness for the last five or possibly fifteen or maybe even sixty minutes. His gentle commentary is beginning to stiffen with imperative. Any minute now, he will pry their eyes open with his grubby little fingers. It's morning again and time to get up.

'Okay, Toby. We're up.' And children are up all over the bulging house: there are kids stashed downstairs and to the right and downstairs and to the left and through the dining room and downstairs again in the basement. Originally, the house had only two bedrooms, just the size for Solly's Auntie Win, who lived alone and liked it. Then Solly and Isobel showed up with a toddler and two babies and took over the big bedroom right away while she moved down to the main floor. Later, they finished the basement, chopping it up into two small bunkrooms, a bathroom and a room for the television and toys. Later again, Solly and some of his students added another bedroom to one side. Once, the house was small and dignified and now it's lumpy with additions and failed architectural experiments, and nooks turn into halls and halls lead nowhere. Once, it had the kind of integrity you get when a single vision is in charge. Now all kinds of single visions bump into each other and overlap and fray at the edges, which is why Isobel can never find the scissors or the Scotch tape or the camera or the *TV Guide*. Some other vision has got there first.

Growing up in this house is a series of moves down and out: out of the bassinet and down the stairs and into a cot, out of the cot and into a bed, out of that bed and down the hall and into another, and out and through the dining room and downstairs again to a bunk and out of the house and gone. Willow left last year to live in tidy splendour in Yaletown with Stephen. Magnolia ran away two years ago and joined a rock band and slept on a bus until she became rich and famous and got her face on the cover of *People*. Ash sleeps at Tara's place half the time.

Isobel gets out of bed, shivers, decides she's definitely pregnant, puts on her very warm robe and her sheepskin slippers and slops downstairs to turn on the heat. Solly gives Toby a big, slobbery, smelly, hairy kiss, jumps out of bed and puts on, as quickly as possible, jeans, a flannel shirt and a very old sweater.

Toby crawls under the covers and giggles.

Solly looks at the bed and yells, 'Isobel, this bed's giggling again!'

'I know,' her voice floats up the stairwell, 'I'll have to get someone in to look at it.'

Solly plucks the covers off the bed and reveals the quivering Toby. He picks him up, holds him at eye level and commands, 'Get dressed. Underpants, socks, T-shirt, sweat shirt, sweat pants. Got it?'

Toby sighs. 'Okay,' he says, 'but I'm warning you, the underpants is a problem. People around here steal my underpants.'

Solly puts him down, spins him around and propels him in the direction of the stairs. 'That's dumb, Tobe, and you know it. Nobody can fit into your underpants. You've got the puniest bum in the whole family.'

Toby begins to hop down the stairs in the slipshod, careless way all the kids have, the way that makes Solly hear sickening smacks against the risers and see crumpled bodies on the landing. Toby turns back to look at him, teeters on one leg and yells, 'You got the stinkiest, though!'

'Just hold onto that banister, boy!' Solly growls. 'What do you think it's there for?'

Toby achieves the base of the stairs without incident and the day dawns on him. 'Halloween!' he hoots. 'Halloween,

Monty!' He races off in search of his little brother.

At a dinner party, a male witch (of the respectable univer-sity-teaching kind) once told Solly that each year, as he watched the little clumps of trick-or-treaters giggle their way down the dark, damp streets, he could see behind them a hideous, cackling mob of ghouls. 'Halloween,' he claimed, 'is a holiday with teeth.' Solly had scoffed, dismissing the man as a pretentious fool. There was enough to fear out there. No need to make things up.

He assesses himself in the mirror while brushing his teeth. He's kept his hair. It's still more black than grey, but he's decided that the grey is going to look all right. He has the kind of broad body and deep chest that can carry extra weight. He's very vain and, because of it, takes great pains to give the impression of a man who isn't. He's ashamed of this trait and believes that no one else knows about it. He's wrong.

He must now go downstairs and out to the garage and put on the coffee and rouse the students and explain to them that things are about to change. 'We all have to grow up sometime, right?' he asks his mirror image.

Although it's as hectic as any other time of day, breakfast has a fixed quality that appeals to Isobel. Children are present and accounted for then; they can be assigned a number.

She pushes toast. Toast does not require a plate. Toast can be eaten standing up. Toast can be prepared and consumed with a minimum of fuss (pop-pop goes the six-slice toaster and another loaf of Marnie's bread is gone). Eggs in any form are off the menu. Even if someone volunteers to cook them, they don't clean the pan afterward, do they? Still, there's always someone who will go hungry without cereal or yogurt, so bowls and spoons are available on request.

In the bay they added to the kitchen five years ago is a round table, which accommodates, with some jostling, six chairs. The toaster stands in the middle of the table. The knives Isobel plunked down at seven are now strewn around it in sticky disarray: strawberry jam, butter, honey, peanut butter – smooth and chunky. The butter dish slides back and forth across the table as if it's riding out a stormy sea.

'Why is it that you can't ever remember to buy margarine?' Winnie's a vegetarian and fussy about food in general. She has recently decided that margarine is better than butter. Isobel promises once again to remember: there is something to be said for food that comes in its own container.

'But you won't. Ever. You always forget.' Winnie is capable of sounding downtrodden and superior at the same time.

Six children sit on six chairs. Since Willow and Maggie are gone, only one has to stand and, in theory anyway, the older children take it in turns. Monty, who believes he has outgrown his high-chair, fidgets about Halloween on top of the Yellow Pages which are flaking away page by page under this strategy. Isobel doesn't have to worry about feeding Monty: the older children keep him supplied with odd corners of toast. The baby is always looked after; it's the former baby she has to watch out for. She hovers over the toaster on Toby's behalf. Toby, at five, hasn't yet developed the killer instinct necessary to snatch a piece of toast and Isobel at forty-five isn't much better. 'Toby gets a piece this time,' she announces, looking hard at Mick, who's quick and unobtrusive and usually gets more than his share. Mick doesn't acknowledge or even seem to realize that he lives in a large family where sharing and taking one's turn are necessary to peaceful coexistence. He's a sturdy boy with Solly's build, at eleven the biggest boy on his soccer team. He's good at math; its precision pleases him: Mick doesn't trust grey areas. Mick, Isobel is convinced, would survive even now if he were cast out into the street. He would still get more than his share of toast. Mick, of course, has obtained a chair.

Monty spills his juice. Isobel grabs a dishcloth and leaps to sop up the remorselessly spreading pool.

'What we really need around here is an absorbent table,'

Ash observes from behind the *Vancouver Sun*.

'With little drainage ditches around the outside. Like eave-stroughing,' Pierre says. 'Hey, what do you think? You think Dad could make it?'

But the furniture Solly builds is so fine and rare that it isn't really furniture any more. No one would dream of allowing apple juice in the vicinity of one of Solly's tables. The kitchen table is made of Arborite by Sears.

The first of the students begin to wander in through the back door, looking less hungry than absent-minded as they palm slices of bread. Some, like Marnie who helps in the house, sleep in the garage but others prefer freedom to safety. Bojo, who has probably walked all the way from his squat in Shaughnessy in his gaping running shoes and who has the wary appearance of a kid with a knife concealed on his person, walks over to the sink, wets a washcloth and gently swabs the jam off Toby's face.

'What's your shoe size, Bojo?' Isobel asks. She'll go through the bins at the high school. Sometimes what Solly hopes will happen with these kids does happen.

'Eat something, Suzannah,' she begs.

Suzannah is tiny for eight and her skin is so transparent you can track the course of her veins. In winter, marks like old bruises appear under her eyes. She's never eaten a complete meal. It's for Suzannah's sake that there's a box of Raisin Bran on the table. Suzannah can't eat toast: she finds it too dry and difficult to chew. Now she waits for the cereal to attain the necessary degree of sog while Toby grabs the box and negotiates the maze on the back with a jammy knife.

Isobel breaks down. 'Suzannah, how about a Christmas orange?' She ate nearly a whole one yesterday. 'I'll take one,' Mick shouts.

'Yeah, I'll go for one,' says Pierre, who's been leaning against the counter reading *The Day of the Triffids* and getting in the way.

So Isobel gets out the ten-dollar box of oranges and in minutes only the two mouldy ones are left and the table is littered with peel and squares of green tissue paper waft around the floor.

'You have to sign this permission slip for the Pumpkin Patch and I need four dollars and thirty-five cents.'

'Who made the lunches? This apple's just one big bruise.'

'Why can't we ever have Fruit Roll-Ups? Sam always has Fruit Roll-Ups. And Sam's mother always makes these fantastic pumpkin cookies for Halloween. What do we get? Apples!'

Isobel is prickly this morning, ready to snap over the spilled juice, the sticky fingers, the students who can only drink coffee, not make it, the tardy leavers, the kid who intends to walk through the pouring rain to the bus stop with no more protection than a T-shirt and jeans. She feels the impulse to snap, slap, scream, she who has become an icon of maternity on the CBC, where her slapdash attitude both reassures and amuses listeners to the 'Family Matters' feature.

And it's Marnie's day off.

'Time's up,' she yells. 'Out! Everybody out who's supposed to go.'

'Sam's mum always drives him to school.'

Isobel holds her breath and counts to ten and prays that Sam and his mother will get their comeuppance one day.

Isobel has a doctor's appointment.

'What are you going to the doctor for?' Solly demands with uncalled-for belligerence. He's told his students he will soon be their employer. He's made his little speech. It didn't feel right. He doesn't need a change in routine today. Besides, he's afraid of going to the doctor. Doctors find things and then poke at them and they get worse.

'Just a check-up,' she says. He's sure she's lying. He takes a good look at her. He hasn't really looked at her for years; ordinarily he sees what he expects to see. She's thin, but not as thin as she was at twenty. She's softened and curved with child-bearing. Slim is a better word for what she is. She's no paler than usual; in Isobel, it's ruddiness you have to worry about. She looks tired as she always does and her skin is taking on the crumpled translucency of a poppy petal. One of his women once described her as a washed-out rag and he hit her for it. That was years ago: he hit the woman not so much for the insult to Isobel as for the insult to him. The rules he applied to sexual freedom didn't allow for jealousy and vindictiveness.

That was a long time ago. He tries to remember the last woman. She was very large, he thinks, and there was something about that monumental size that fascinated him. Could he reach her centre? Would she make use of her greater strength? Would she writhe and buck? The possibility had been irresistible.

Solly can look at bodies all day. He studies perfection and oddity with equal affection. He loves the disproportion of new-born babies and very old men. When he encounters an anatomical curiosity– an extra toe, a hunchback, a more than average lack of symmetry – he will pursue it, observe it from all angles, measure it, even feel it if he gets the chance. And he usually does; the deformed prefer his overt interest to the affected indifference they usually encounter. Yes, the last woman was vast and possessed, he remembers, of a laugh as rich as gravy. For the last, she was a good choice. She was a year ago. This is amazing.

It wasn't guilt, it wasn't fear, it wasn't ennui or failing energy that made him stop. He hadn't really stopped at all, just not started again.

He shrinks from the thought of how easily he might have let Isobel go; how he nearly ran away, how he dared her to leave him, how, when she screamed and ranted or sank into depression, he almost threw her out. Go, he had said, you're free. But she had clung and stayed. How highly he valued her freedom, how cheaply her continued presence.

When she returns from the doctor, he pulls her toward him and tucks her into his flank where she fits like the best joinery. He cups her head in his hand and kisses her fading hair. The last streaks of yellow and gold look darker now against the encroaching white. Her bones are holding well, though, as he had known they would. He finds her very beautiful now; as a girl she'd been outshone by women of more obvious and transitory appeal. He remembers all the prettier, easier girls he had while Isobel stood by.

'What did she say?'

'The usual,' she says. She's not looking herself in make-up and a sleeveless dress that shows off limbs as beautifully turned as the legs of a Queen Anne chair.

'What do you mean, the usual?' he asks. Isobel isn't ordinarily playful. It doesn't suit her. And she never goes to the doctor so there isn't a usual.

'Just the same thing I've had eight times before,' she says with a smile like a flourish. 'She's running the test, but I'm sure.' Then the children hear her and thunder in, the little boys pelting her with their bodies and Mick saying 'Mum, Mum' at ten-second intervals while Suzannah performs a perfect cartwheel in a sliver of space between two chairs and Winnie asks what's for dinner and Ash waits ostentatiously for his turn.

'Curried vegetables or curried vegetables with tiny pieces of chicken for the evil carnivores. Did somebody slice the vegetables? Did anybody check the Halloween candy? I know I told somebody to do that. Did you get my note? Where's Pierre?'

'Soccer. He's got his bike.' Solly says, falling without effort into the ordinariness of it all when he should, of course, be shocked into silence.

An hour later, Isobel struggles out of the van in the pouring rain with three kids and several last-minute-panic bags of candy. Pumpkins are already lit and the early, tiny trick-or-treaters are skittering along the sidewalk like blown leaves. The crowd of reporters is back and it's huge, although the tour is long gone. What has Maggie done now?

She grabs the kids and puts her head down and curses Magnolia and her terrible fame.

An overnight success, Solly has called it scornfully. 'She'll be old news in five minutes. Wait and see.'

Mrs Whitechapel?

Mrs Whitechapel?

Isobel?

Ms Lamb?

Mrs Whitechapel, can you give us your response to the story on Dirt Tonite?

'Will you please let us through? The kids are getting soaked.'

Mrs Whitechapel. Do you deny that you kidnapped Magnolia White when she was a baby and have posed as her birth mother ever since?

She stops.

'Do I what? What? Do I what?'

'I said, do you deny that you kidnapped ...'

Her mouth has dropped open. Rain plasters her pale hair to her skull and pours down her face. She looks bald and wet and addled. She knows this because she sees herself later on the dinner hour news. Even the *Sun* prints a still photo on the front page the following morning. Even the CBC has deemed it newsworthy. It becomes a moment that will last forever.

There is that frozen moment of comprehension before she comes to her senses, booms GET OUT OF OUR WAY and fixes the reporters with the steely eye she has honed for years against the rough insouciance of adolescents. The press fall back and let her pass; they have caught the crucial moment of discovery anyway and have the sense to wait until she's slammed the front door before addressing their cameras and describing her as distraught, an observation which will later accompany footage of her looking insane.

Halloween.

Magnolia's itinerary has vanished. Isobel is almost sure she stuck it on the fridge. She hasn't needed it before. It's always Maggie who calls, never Isobel.

'Get Daddy quick!' she shrieks at Suzannah. 'How should I know? In the studio!'

Solly storms in, fear in his throat, expecting spurting arteries, unconsciousness, sudden death.

'She knows,' Isobel says.

'Knows what?' asks Toby, who has been left in his coat and boots and is afraid of this mother.

'Nothing. Suzannah, sweetheart, get their things off, okay?' She pulls bags of candy out of a cupboard, finds a mixing bowl. 'How about you guys fill the bowl for the trick-or-treaters, eh?'

Solly manhandles her into the dining room.

'Knows what? Who knows?'

'Maggie.'

He understands, of course, and feels the first spurt of rage. He drops his hands from her shoulders and quickly steps away from her. Isobel has no idea how close she's just come to harm or how many times in the past he's had to step back like this, draw breath, unfist his hands. He's a hero in his way.

'Where is she? Have you called?'

'I can't find the sheet. Can you remember where the Halloween concert was?'

Magnolia called last night.

What're you going to be for Halloween?

The Queen of the Dead.

Oh, what does that look like?

Me.

Oh Maggie.

In no time at all the kids troop back into the dining room.

'Okay, we've done that. Can we get into our costumes yet? And you're supposed to do the UNICEF boxes, remember?'

'Yup. Right. You guys go and watch TV, okay?'

They're shocked. 'But it's still afternoon.'

'Well, but it's a holiday.'

'No, it isn't. Halloween isn't a holiday. It's a pagan festival.' Suzannah is a pedant. 'Oh, all right.' She sighs and wanders off.

The little boys won't go though, not even for television. They're afraid to leave their parents in such a state. These are new parents and not to be trusted. They demand to be held and spoken to softly.

Solly looks suddenly old over Monty's curly head. 'She'll call,' he says. 'It'll be all right.'

Halloween. The unmasking. The more thoughtful of the television pundits don't miss the analogy. Coincidence must be made to have meaning. Great stories are made of timeliness, pathos and nasty surprise.

None of this occurs to Solly and Isobel. Not yet. At the end of that long day they lie with barely enough energy to warm the covers and stare up at the grimy sloping ceiling. Magnolia has cancelled concerts and disappeared somewhere in Iowa. Vanished. Gone. Imagine that. That's what they think of. And what do they talk of? Little things.

Isobel says, 'I had way too much candy. I hate that. You remember last year we had tons left over too? I thought I'd compensated. You'd think after all these years I'd get it right.'

'They were avoiding the house. Who'd send kids through that mob out there? Besides, there are fewer kids every year. Parents aren't letting them go out any more. It's too dangerous. Don't you read the paper? They have special supervised parties instead.'

'Dangerous!' Isobel explodes. He's hit a nerve. 'Yet another danger for the poor little things to fret over. Dangerous to talk to the old man at the park! Dangerous to play on the sidewalk in front of your own house! Dangerous to ride your bike around the block! Why not just wrap them in cotton batting and shut them away in a nice safe vault?'

'But it *is* dangerous. You don't seem to get that! God, imagine the parents! What would we do? I can't stand even to think about it.' Then he remembers that he *is* the parent of a missing child and stops talking for fear of imagining.

Solly and Isobel have been together for twenty-five years; more than long enough for them to have amassed a list of topics about which argument is futile. The relative safety of the world is one of them. Isobel insists that the world is no more dangerous now than it was when, as a child, she took the bus to dentist's appointments and swimming lessons, rode her bike all over town and disappeared from breakfast to dinner. Solly, whose childhood was well cushioned by money and privilege, believes that evil pervades the outside world and that the slightest crack in security will allow it to seep inside like poison gas. With every child he becomes more fearful, and the inevitable near misses, lucky escapes, nasty falls, high fevers, and short-term disappearances of children nurture in him an unbearable dread; it visits him in quiet moments and whispers how uncannily lucky he has been so far. To keep the dread away, he has kept his hands full of tools and good, sound wood and (until recently) warm comforting flesh; his mind full of large and complex schemes.

Isobel is too occupied with the momentary present to entertain tragedy in a theoretical form. Magnolia has vanished somewhere in Iowa. Magnolia, the child she saved. Magnolia of the melancholy DNA.

'We should have told her,' he says. 'We should have told her years ago.'

'But she was always so sensitive. So unstable. Ordinary life was hard.'

'She's stable now? Jesus, I'm cold!' Solly shivers and pulls her against him. He's taken the little ones out trick-or-treating and has spent too long standing guard on the sidewalk in the raw damp air that chills but never numbs. The children have come home glittering with excitement and have either eaten too much junk or gloated over it according to their natures, and have been more than usually tiresome about going to bed.

Solly closes his eyes and tries not to see Magnolia's face. He wants more than anything to go to sleep. There are answers in sleep and dreaming. He's found them before.

Isobel wriggles. 'Did you actually get that I'm pregnant?' she asks peevishly.

She hears him groan and waits for him to say what he always says. They have too many children already and she's too old, which is true, she almost was too old. Month after month she has been not pregnant. Now she is. But this will be her last baby. She's made up her mind about that. She needs this baby now. She's soft and single-minded when pregnant. She becomes large and important. Men hold her in awe. When breast-feeding, she's round and padded at the corners; after weaning, she's a shrivelled, faded little woman. In another age, she'd have had twelve children and thought nothing of it. In the age of family planning, her fecundity seems self-indulgent, politically motivated and not in the best of taste.

She waits, tucked into his warmth. He hasn't stiffened or moved away, but the fury is there, she can feel it. He seems to be holding his breath.

'I haven't slept with another woman in a year, did you know that?'

'No,' she answers, shocked. 'How could I know?' She's made so many tiny shifts in perception over so many years; she's edged from shrieking jealousy and paralytic depression to numb acknowledgement. She's walled it off and, now that he claims to have stopped, she's disconcerted.

She changes the subject.

'I thought I saw Auntie Win today,' she says.

'Oh, for Christ's sake,' he mutters. He'll never get to sleep.

'Honestly. No kidding. I'm sure I saw her. Right there at the top of the stairs. I was carrying some laundry along the hall past the landing and I saw her out of the corner of my eye. She was standing right there. And I just kept on walking, sort of on automatic, you know the way you do. By the time I'd stopped and gone back, she wasn't there.'

'Well, of course she wasn't there. You're imagining things,' Solly says as he tries to think back to the beginning of February or thereabouts.

'I wouldn't mind her as a ghost, would you? I always liked the ghosts at the Farm. I mean as long as she wasn't headless or something and frightened the kids. Auntie Win would be fine. I forget her. I forget her all the time. It's like she was never really here. I called her name – you know – the way you do when you're not sure if someone's asleep, just softly in case you might disturb them. I came up here and looked for her, but she was gone and it wasn't even cold, not any colder than usual. Aren't ghosts supposed to leave a place cold?'

But by now Solly, unable to remember February or thereabouts, has finally escaped into sleep and Isobel looks at Auntie Win's portrait and rolls her eyes.

She sits up and watches Solly sleep. She's never recovered from being in love with him, the way you're supposed to; the attachment becoming comfortable and easy; she still feels the aching tenuousness of the connection. He grunts as she smooths his hair, just as he always does. This, at least, is the same. She's not sure she can handle any more changes.

She knows that, outside, the vans and helicopters are converging, the lights are being set up. Somewhere out there, the reporters are doing their hair. In the morning, they'll have her for breakfast.

Chapter Four

It was once the fashion to remember the womb. 'Warm,' people would say. 'It was really warm.' Or dark. Or red. Or wet. They were so tickled with themselves to have remembered.

The Famous Frances, in her prime at the time and moving in womb-ridden circles, would flick back her henna'd hair and snort like a horse: 'I'll believe it when you say there was a Van Gogh print on the wall and the ashtrays needed emptying.' It was this kind of statement that got her name in the papers, not her noisy despair of the past but her brisk contempt for the trends of the present.

Solly said he couldn't stand to think of wombs; they were too closely linked to birth and the thought of birth might put him off sex and then where would he be? 'Think of it, it's like a Mack truck going through there,' he said. (Isobel didn't believe him. She knew it was fear that kept him away. He watched Willow's delivery before he knew any better; once was enough. Now she mangles the hand of some obliging nurse. She thinks the world of nurses.)

Isobel tried to remember the womb and listened with interest to those who did because she suspected that, having reached so far back to their primitive beginnings, they had touched a mystery, accomplished something beyond a mere feat of memory or imagination.

Her own babies, all eight of them, emerged with startled expressions on their faces. They looked at her hard. They coolly appraised her. She wondered if her outside measured up to her in. She's pale and angular on the outside, not a comfortable prospect after the utter plush of that warm, red room.

Her memory begins at the age of six when her youngest sister was born. She could paint that scene: the focal point a grunting, fluffy little parcel, the navy blue chair, the weirdly angular flowers on the Axminster rug; in the foreground, in descending size, Bob and Isobel and Laura emitting yellow slashes of outrage at being made to wait for their lunch while this greedy little interloper has hers. Her mother is just a shape in memory, just a shape holding the baby, not really registered at all, as if there was no need to see her; she was a constant unworthy of record, neither young as she was then nor old as she is now. Just there, as always.

She can't understand why this event has lodged in her brain, when a year earlier she broke her collarbone and of that she remembers nothing. It seems she has a magpie memory which picks up glittery bits of trivia but leaves behind the large events as too onerous to carry. And she knows there's more to memory than the straightforward recording of event. She has *déjà vu* for certain places. She will catch a glimpse out of a car window of an old shingled house, a yardful of long, yellow summer grass and the leaves of an aspen lifted by a quick wind and she will yearn for that place as for an old home.

Among the many forgotten days is the day her father ran away from home. This is how her mother describes it still. He didn't leave. He didn't abandon them. He ran away. (Perhaps her memory is impaired by the cartoon image of the little boy with his belongings tied up in a rag at the end of a stick.) Frances uses the term 'running way' in the sense of 'from his responsibilities' because responsibility is a trait Frances reveres in herself and others.

And Isobel doesn't remember that day. She doesn't remember a day when she realized that Daddy was gone forever. He was gone all the time anyway, for work. Like every father she knew, he worked for the government. That was what fathers did in Ottawa in 1961, when there were all kinds of government for whom fathers could work. He works for the government, they would say in the schoolyard, quickly establishing themselves within the essential parameters of normalcy.

Isobel's father worked discreetly for External Affairs. Anonymity was his particular gift. He was unnoticeable against any background, including his own, which is perhaps why she can't picture him now.

There are times, of course, when her children ask about him, their grandfather, and Isobel has to build a man from scraps. He had a green thumb. He had a gift for languages; that's why you're good at French.

Frances is no help. *I don't remember. He's dead by now, what does it matter? Let him go.*

Although he has now been gone for most of her life, she doesn't feel she's lost him. He's there somewhere. When perestroika happened, she waited for the phone call. She still watches documentary films that feature out-of-the-way settings: New Guinea, Magadan, Liberia. Whenever a third attaché is expelled in disgrace, she thinks of her father, a blurred shape at the edge of a snapshot, a word stuck forever on the tip of the tongue.

She keeps track of Missing Persons in the paper. If they're men, they'll get off a plane, check into a hotel, use the phone to arrange business meetings for the following morning and then become Missing. Their absence will take a day or two to register but eventually a story will appear in the paper and a worried brother or father, rarely a wife, will show up, hoping for amnesia.

If they're women, they're usually dead — occasionally insane, but usually dead. Women don't run away frivolously, it seems. Sometimes a woman will be Missing for years and then a hiker will trip over a tibia and she'll just be Dead.

That her first fatherless day is unmarked in memory is to the credit of her now famous mum, Frances, who hadn't yet let out her anger and was still hoarding it in her girdle (which she once wore, Isobel is prepared to swear to it). When the children asked, as they must have done from time to time, when Daddy was coming home, she kept her tone calm and unremarkable so they sidled into fatherlessness unaware that they were moving at all. He had been a remote man when present, uninvolved even on the coaching/camping/fishing level that most fathers aspired to. There were few significant events from which he could unequivocally be identified as missing.

'What do fathers do?' Isobel's brother Bob, long-distance, in a panic after the birth of his first child.

'How should I know what they do? Just don't disappear. That's the main thing.'

Isobel's strongest memories of her father are, in fact, memories of her mother. She can see her in a gingham apron telling Bob that they can't have beans because Dad hates them: he had to eat too many during the war. She can see her coming up the basement stairs with a sack of dahlia tubers; she can remember being taught how to separate the sausagy roots, an eye to each, and later filling big holes with manure, then watering and feeding and staking the sappy, muscular plants that were said to be his favourites, but she can't recall her father admiring them and she certainly doesn't remember the autumn day they weren't dug up but were left in the ground to freeze and rot.

It was the fashion not to tell unpalatable truths to children but to smooth routine over disaster like icing on a cracked cake. And the children didn't dare to ask after him. If fathers could go missing then surely mothers could too, especially when bothered by too many questions. So they quietly swallowed the cake and almost enjoyed the icing. (Of course, these days sugar-coating is not recommended no matter how bitter the truth it conceals, and these days Isobel sometimes regrets the loss of that sweet masquerade.)

By the time they dared to ask questions, Frances had had some months of recovery and adjustment in which to make a tidy shape of her husband's vanishing. He'd only been a husband, after all. Unlike fathers, husbands could be replaced. She'd already lost one to war and he'd been easy enough to erase. She'd decided that this one, who'd seemed at first profound and fascinating and became as time passed odd and unpredictable, disappearing without explanation for reasons to do with work, less and less involved with her own life which was at the time firmly practical, to do with bills and food and children's shoes and homework and house-cleaning; she decided that he hadn't abruptly vanished like the first one, but had worn away like a softstone carving left out in all weathers so its features gradually melt until they are undiscernible and forgotten, the stone now given import only by the prominence of its position.

Now she has Marcel and she loves him fondly but with reservation, too wise to risk a gaping wound should he suddenly vanish. She frets about Isobel who loves Solly so recklessly, with such a raw exposed passion she wants to sear it with mercurochrome and swaddle it in Elastoplast.

Frances was angry when Duncan didn't return from that last trip. His running away had nothing to do with her; it was all about him. Still, a vanished man brings home no bacon, makes no car or house payments. A vanished man is downright scary when it comes time to pay the bills. 'He couldn't cope; that was all,' she told the children finally. 'He was never good at the everyday. I can't tell you more than that. That's all I know. It might have been the war. He didn't talk about it. I imagine he's dead by now, anyway. He really couldn't cope. *I* was the coper.'

And now when Isobel asks, so many years later, 'But why did he run away?'

'Oh, I don't know and I no longer care. He was forty-six. Not a good age in a man. Don't start looking for patterns. There aren't any.'

'Was it something he found out? Why didn't he come back?'

This is something Isobel remembers; that people run away and they don't come back.

She used to fret over unidentified bodies: there were so many of them – who were they? Whole bodies, former people, who were not even worth claiming, like single mittens. She tried once, when she was twelve, to identify a body, but the police wouldn't let her. *Go home and fetch your mother*, they said. But she couldn't do that. It was too much to ask a grown-up.

It was not really done to have a father missing in those days. Her parents' generation were survivors: of the Holocaust, the Blitz, the War, the Dust Bowl, the Depression, events so awful they were capitalized, and what these survivors most desired for their children were stability and prosperity and above all calm, a condition commonly summed up as 'nice'. Nice was how things were to be kept, whether they were children or lawns or national policy. So carefully did the survivors swaddle their children in niceness that by the time these children were old enough to sneer at it, they had no idea that the opposite of nice shoes from Murphy Gamble was no shoes at all and that the nice new couch so laughably preserved under plastic replaced another that had been abandoned, looted, or blown to pieces.

Isobel could remember her own mother, yes, the Famous Frances Lamb herself, speaking with contempt of another housewife whose beds were unmade at 10 a.m. Frances denies this now, of course. Thirty years later, it does seem unlikely. Isobel is pretty sure Mick's bed hasn't been made since she last changed the sheets and she has a terrible feeling that that was in the spring of '94.

The Famous Frances once said: 'We smothered our shrieks and murmured assent. We had babies, not jobs; we made beds, not deals.' The Famous Frances, once she became famous, often spoke this way even in ordinary conversation, in short, quotable phrases and slogans. When she was only a mother, she wasn't memorable: a pretty woman, plump with fatigue and children's leftovers, struggling to keep her heavy brown hair off her face. Now, at sixty-eight, she has a stagy, exaggerated appearance. Her hair is maroon with henna and cropped short and carelessly combed. Her soft plumpness has solidified, the better for accosting cabinet ministers. Her legs have grown thick with firm planting, her knees are permanently braced, her chin thrust, her finger pointed. Her sensible shoes are heavy, made for marching and stamping off in disgust and, once, for throwing at a Toronto columnist. She wears clear, bright Crayola colours you can pick out across a room. She has made a personage of herself.

Even now, Frances has her supporters, although the bright, glittering, driven ones have moved on and up, as they will, to success and complacency. (Having achieved equality themselves, they tend to defend the struggle as character-building.) Those who remain are bitter with sour experience and well-nourished grudges. When these women form her entourage, they have the impervious, narrow perception of bodyguards. Frances fought for a woman's right to do anything she chose, and when Isobel chose to become a chicken-soup-making, bread-baking mother of nine, there was resentment among the acolytes, who felt this wasn't playing fair. Privately, they call her Dizzy Izzy, part courtesan, part wet-nurse, a kept woman who can't possibly understand Frances. Sometimes, she wants to scream at these women: 'She's not Frances Lamb to me; to me she's Mother!' But this, of course, is exactly why they condemn her, while she thinks she sees the truth, ugly and uncompromising as it is: that the public Frances is merely a useful idea and that mothers never, ever, practise what they preach. The acolytes would prefer Frances to be pure and clean, to have sacrificed her personal life to her public one, in the necessarily ruthless manner of all saints and martyrs.

Frances's time is past. Isobel has noticed that real, up-to-the-minute feminists are more likely to take you out to dinner than to throw it at you. Her mother's ideological daughters speak softly and carry writs. It has become fashionable among women of Isobel's age, powerful women now, to disparage the Franceses. They're like hassocks: those round, vinyl-covered, sawdust-stuffed fifties footstools that were once (but never now) called poufs; cheap, ugly things which, though still sturdy enough to stand on to reach the top shelf, no longer go with the furniture and should have been hauled off to the Sally Ann long ago.

But, of course, these clever women were not witnesses to Frances's remarkable evolution.

At first, there was only inertia. For months she and the children drifted on the momentum of breakfast, lunch and dinner, weekdays and weekends, swimming lessons on Mondays and Wednesdays (and snapping off icicles of frozen hair at the bus stop across from the Plante Bath), fewer meat dinners, the car used less and less, but still ordinary, ordinary.

Later, when she wrote her book, Frances would glorify her collapse as a cocoon phase, the essential shapelessness at the centre of a transformation. To her children, she became the shameful mother who wore her dressing gown to drive them to school. The girls sat in the back seat and looked out the window, afraid to look in the front in case Frances had vanished altogether and there was no driver at all. They made her let them out a block away from the convent so that no one would see that she wasn't ordinary any more.

It became vitally important to be ordinary. Isobel began to study the detail of normalcy; elastic bands to hold up knee socks, proper sandwich fillings, the exact placement of barrettes. Who would have thought that skinny little Isobel, always the head of the class, her curtsey as she crossed the path of a nun the proper balance between reverence and flattery, a shoo-in to give the speech to Mme Vanier even if the prime minister's niece *was* in the class, wings of fine white hair sweeping as she bent over her *dictée*, as she mastered the definition of *archipelago* (firmly mispronounced ar-cha-pi-lay-go by the nuns and thus a word Isobel would be forced to avoid for the rest of her life even when she lived in one); who would have thought that Isobel strove so hard for banality? That old Sister Margaret ringing her bell at the school gate, the byzantine code of behaviour, the unfailing routine and calm order of the convent represented an asylum from anarchy?

At home, for how long she can't remember, the children bought milk, made beds and cookies, vacuumed, emptied heaped ashtrays. Meals appeared early or late or not at all. Dirty clothes lay in damp piles on the floor or were so elaborately laundered that they didn't dare disturb them. The other mothers on the street began to notice and singled the children out for absurdly petty compliments: their nice, straight noses, excellent posture, the tidy partings of their hair.

Then, overnight it seemed, Frances changed and the house went up for sale and the car too and the girls were quite old enough to go to school on the bus and who cared what the nuns thought? The nuns were an anachronistic coven of snobs anyway. And they left the post-war brick bungalow in the West End, on the street where everyone had a father who worked for the government and a second car and a basement finished in knotty pine and a permed-and-set mother who made dessert, and moved downtown to the narrow wooden house with the crooked front steps that emptied onto the sidewalk on a street where the cooking smells were funny and no one spoke English or French, where the women wore kerchiefs and flat shoes and cleaned other people's houses and made their children practise the piano for hours. Now, if they wanted, the children could say my *mother* works for the government. But they never did.

Now Frances is old and Isobel has a cheating husband she would kill for and a missing child and a cluster of dubious hangers-on and it could be said that beyond the basic reproductive function, Frances' life achievement has had no bearing on her daughter.

'Done any painting?' Frances will ask, tossing it in at the end of a long distance phone call. (Not that it matters. It's your life.)

'Not lately,' Isobel will answer. She isn't a painter. She's no more a painter than her friend Pat, who goes to the gym every day, is an athlete.

Still, she admires the shape of her brushes fanned out in a peanut butter jar in the laundry room, the thick luxury of the paper; she enjoys the discipline of all those tiny ordered marks, the exactness of it all, the stifling of the creative impulse that is botanic art. That she has chosen the least plastic field in painting is not surprising: children are so plastic.

The Famous Frances says Isobel's pictures are pretty, by which she means bad. She sees this passive recording of the ephemeral, this concentration on accuracy as an enshrinement of the insignificant. At best, she feels that Isobel's paintings are pleasant accessories, the kind of thing people without souls hang in clusters on their dining room walls. She wants surly slashes of red on black backgrounds. Once, when Isobel was painting a miniature day lily she'd raised from seed, working desperately to catch the flower before it crumpled, Frances seized on the image. 'Yes,' she said. 'Yes! The brief beauty of the flower! Only the roots have meaning; they are the real thing, the source of life.'

'Actually, the beauty has meaning too – at least to the plant it does. Without the flower there wouldn't be seed. Flowers are necessary too.'

'I see,' Frances said, 'is that your statement, then? That the beauty, no matter how short-lived, exists for a reason? Then you could paint in a crumpled flower behind.'

'This variety drops its faded blossoms. But I could paint in a seed pod. That's only beautiful in an ugly, practical way.'

'Right, now I've got it. The dry husk of vitality.' And Frances strode off, feeling much better, the statement made, leaving Isobel to contemplate the sketch of the pretty little plant in its game last flowering and all those promising seeds in the pod.

Chapter Five

Solly entered a room. Isobel fell in love. They drove across the country in a car named Rex and so we are here.

This is what the children say, or what they would say if they bothered – the story is ingrained from their earliest childhood, such an intrinsic part of their collective memory that it might now be called instinct. Just as they will someday know, without knowing, how to comfort a fussy baby, so they know that love is easy and immediate and that it changes your life. Family myths are like that: too simple and straightforward to be anything but sophistry.

She met him at Anne's cottage. It was the end of August and the last of the sticky teenage summers she'd wasted refolding sweaters for minimum wage in a fashion boutique on the Sparks Street Mall. She would be at Queen's in two weeks. Marcel had found her a room there and a part-time job as a ward maid at the Hotel Dieu. Isobel couldn't wait. She was seventeen. She had Latin, English, French, Maths A and B, Physics, Biology, Chemistry, History. She'd won a scholarship; she'd been an exceptionally good child, and now it was time to begin her real life and cut herself free from her family, just as Frances had trained her to do. Isobel had listened too well to her mother's speeches and had mistaken cant for personal conviction. She truly believed her mother would understand that now was Isobel's time and that she wanted to be a painter not a lawyer. Let Laura and Faye be the lawyers and fight the family battles. (Bob had already dropped out of sociology at Carlton and become a garbage man, swaggering over an immense hourly wage, more than Frances herself made *and what skills does he need? a strong back and a good pair of gloves!* If Isobel had listened to Frances rave about that one, she would have known better.)

Now she would finally learn to draw and paint. She hoped she was not already too old to learn. She would study the masters, slide after slide of them, and take notes and make sketches and be above washing her hair. She would fall secretly in love with a professor, possibly seduce him, absorb from him a cool maturity and move on.

Frances had a fit. 'Straight A's!' she screamed. 'A scholarship!' Her lover, Marcel, had to make her tea and feed her chocolate. 'You must allow Isobel to do what she wishes now,' he murmured. 'Let her go and perhaps she will come back. She has been such a good girl for you. In any case, she will need some kind of undergraduate degree to get into law school.'

'In art?' Frances shrieked.

Stunned, she permitted Isobel to quit work two weeks early to go to Anne's cottage, although she had always disapproved of Anne's parents who were rich and privileged and hadn't, she claimed, entertained a new idea since the Family Compact. (Because of this, Frances had always been particularly nice to Anne, making a special effort as she might for a member of an endangered species.)

Anne was Isobel's opposite, as girlfriends so often are, a spirited, rich girl of easy and indiscriminate affection. ('She treats her like a pet!' Frances had complained to Marcel. 'A much loved pet. You underestimate Anne. She is lazy, but kind and good. Isobel has fun with her. Isobel needs to have fun.')

They had been best friends since grade one and they read each other's minds. They were big and small, brunette and blonde, outgoing and withdrawn, people-smart and school-smart, like sisters without the competition, like lovers without the sex. Isobel explained *Othello* to Anne. Anne explained petting to Isobel. They fought and forgot, they abetted one another in silly schemes, they spoke their own language. They couldn't imagine a future apart. They imagined falling in love; they imagined it all the time, but they would fall in love with brothers or best friends or not at all. They wished away the unthinkable, which was separation. Theirs was the strongest bond they recognized.

They played the 'game of love'. What would you do for love? they asked each other. Would you die to save your lover? Oh, yes. Would you steal if your children were starving? Oh yes, yes.

Anne lived in a big dark house full of grubby priceless furniture and, though her much married parents had produced an enormous confusion of step and half and full siblings, the house was always cool and empty; it demanded whispered conversation and quiet, tidy play. A snack requested from the kitchen arrived, potato chips all right, but in a silver bowl on a linen napkin and a tray, so that Isobel felt the need to let the chips grow limp and silent in her mouth before chewing them. They preferred to play at Isobel's house, which smelled of overbrewed coffee and smouldering cigarettes and was frequently full of loud, indignant women and foreign languages. There were never potato chips at Isobel's house, but you could eat graham crackers right out of the box without shame.

So Isobel was released from the boutique two weeks before she was due at Queen's. Her mother, seized by a surprisingly bourgeois anxiety, rushed out to the Hudson's Bay to buy new underwear and a shorts-and-top set in orange crimplene, which Isobel wore with a certain smug assurance on the milk-run bus to North Bay. She adhered to the vinyl seat for seven hours with her purse and suitcase wedged between her feet as the bus jolted out of the Ottawa Valley and into the Canadian Shield: stopping at Bell's Corners, Renfrew, Algonquin Park, onto the main highway at Huntsville and into North Bay. She had no choice but to study the landscape, which of course had already been done. The Group of Seven were out of fashion. Paint by numbers, she had once called them, being smart and upsetting her grade eight teacher. Before her now were Jacksons and Thomsons, simple shapes in jaded, late summer colours.

She felt too good for the milk-run in her new orange outfit among the fat, rumpled young mothers and the travelling men in their sad, shiny suits; that is, until she saw Anne, who showed up late to meet her in espadrilles gone through at the toe, no bra and boy's shorts two sizes too large, at which point she suddenly felt too new, too cheap, too fashionable, too orange.

'It doesn't matter,' Anne said, ashamed of herself for laughing. 'Who cares? No one at camp cares what they look like.'

Which was as true as most truths. But they didn't care the way the old rich don't care. Every washed-out, tattered rag spoke of plenty of money spent long ago. If moccasin seams gaped it was because they were hand-sewn; these were the best gapes money could buy. Raised to be above caring, Isobel found she cared a lot. She hadn't known of the existence of this confident race or that Anne was a member of it. At the convent, there had been the levelling effect of the school uniform, and a rather cruel emphasis on the academic that favoured girls like Isobel over girls like Anne.

When she was younger, her mother had twice rented cabins on the Ottawa River, and Isobel had come to define the concept of the summer cottage by those splintery, listing shacks which smelled of propane and inadequate sewage treatment. The swimming was good once you got past the weeds into deep water, but Isobel was terrified of the weeds and even more terrified when briskly warned against panicking; a person who panicked and thrashed in the weeds could wind herself up in their slimy clinging fingers and be drowned by her own fear. She preferred to stay inside the cottages with the frail card tables and incomplete jigsaw puzzles, the ancient, limp magazines which had the scoop on what had once been the latest thing, the furniture which smelled of other people and their foibles.

She was frightened by Anne's cottage, a picturesque scattering of log buildings over acres of discreetly groomed nature. The lake was clean and rock-bottomed: you could jump off the dock into ten feet of clear water. If you were brave (and this was expected) you could jump off the boathouse roof.

She was introduced to an alarming mob of uncles and aunts, cousins and step-grandmothers and half-second-cousins, more a convention than a family. She was given a tour by Anne's father, who waved vaguely at a cabin on a point and muttered something about Varley but who seemed more proud of the big old wood range in the kitchen. Two women from the village cooked all the meals in this furnace, sweat pouring down their faces as they basted turkeys and baked pies. Their names were Kit and Mary. Mother and daughter, they were almost identical; it was difficult to tell who was the mother – they were both heavy, sturdy women with small, pretty features and fine, strawberry blonde hair. One had had the other at fifteen and, at the same age, the other had had another, and now the latest child behaved herself in a playpen in a corner of the immense kitchen. Sometimes, they'd sit on the stoop, which caught the breeze from the lake, and lift their back hair off their necks and their skirts off their thighs and fan their reddened faces with sections of the *Globe and Mail*. Kit and Mary took home laundry every night and returned it clean and stiff with line drying. Their husbands mended roofs and varnished Criscrafts and 'opened' and 'closed' the cottages. In winter, they convalesced and enjoyed a rich and giddy social life that would have shocked their employers.

'Can I help?' Isobel asked the first day, anxious to establish that she too understood manual labour, had washed other people's dishes and put her fingers into other people's food. 'No, honey,' said Kit (or Mary) firmly. 'You just stay right out of our way. I got biscuits for thirty here and those eggs are getting cold.' The camp children were not allowed in the kitchen but it was one of their jobs, when the meal bell rang, to line up and receive trays from these women, which they carried to the dining hall a hundred yards away. This at least gave them some appreciation for the amount of food they ate, pounds and pounds and pounds of it, all served up in special covered dishes and lugged through the woods.

Amusements followed a schedule at Anne's cottage. Rituals were observed. When the kids jumped screaming and soapy into the lake before breakfast, they were maintaining an ancestral tradition. The fire in the great hall was to be lit at five and the oil lamps at nightfall. The great hall smelled of woodsmoke and mousebait and mildew. It was as cold and beautiful as a basilica and refused to surrender from its massive log bones the chill of the long northern winter.

The Munros were conscientious hosts and they mistook Isobel's dazzled sluggishness for timidity. No sooner had she found a comfortable chair than someone dragged her off to have fun. There was never nothing to do. The drinking water had to be fetched from a spring across the lake; there were dishes to be cleared, berries to be picked, canoes to be raced, water to be skied, Sunfish to be sailed, errands to be run at top speed in roaring motorboats. Implicit in the spartan sleeping cabins with their lack of books and reading lamps was the understanding that only a poor sport or a lazybones would want to sit inside and sketch when summer glared just outside the sticky pine door.

There were parties every night. Sometimes they were grownup parties at which the children were expected to be polite and helpful but otherwise could do as they pleased, which meant drinking a lot and taking regular outings to the boathouse in small groups to smoke joints, reappearing fragrant and silly, but still capable of politeness and usefulness when called upon. In Frances's house, there would have been high-pitched lectures, ultimatums and major groundings over such irresponsible behaviour but here a lapse in courtesy or charm was the only punishable transgression.

To watch them, you'd never have known that Anne and Isobel were waiting for Solly. Anne was sure, *well, pretty sure – anyway she hoped* that Solly was coming, *she would die if he didn't.* They contrived to call her brother Michael three times from the village store. He would bring Solly on Saturday. *Was he sure he was coming?* Yes and Saturday was the day. *They'd be there in time for the party?* Yes, definitely.

Anne was consumed with Solly. They'd made love, as she called it, savouring the phrase like an exotic spice, in the back of a car when she was in Toronto visiting Michael. Solly was older, mature, *not like those jerky high school boys from Saint Pat's with their anxious Adam's apples and bad skin.* Solly was hitting the road; he'd had it up to here with U of T. *No, stupid, not Europe, everybody does Europe. Out West to join a commune.*

During the week before he came, Anne built a fine future for herself Out West with Solly and Isobel handed her the mortar, the way girlfriends do, shored up her doubts, supported her desires, applied whispered reassurance in the cold dark cabin, wishing true love on Anne with a grateful shudder. An artist can't afford to fall in love.

Saturday came and Anne prepared herself all afternoon, taking as long to look clean and shiny and natural as her stepsisters had five years before to look hard-eyed and bouffant. Isobel supervised and brushed her teeth and tied back her fine white hair and rehearsed what she would say to Anne's parents when Anne ran away with Solly.

'It was love at first sight.'

Or: *'She said she couldn't live without him.'*

But probably: *'I tried to talk her out of it. She wouldn't listen to me.'*

They were playing *Sergeant Pepper* when he came in. (When Isobel tells her friends they were playing *Sergeant Pepper* when she first saw Solly, they understand.)

The first thing she noticed was that he was a man not a boy, finished and whole and strong without the raw, messy, mid-renovation look of adolescence. Solly isn't as big as he seems but he's broad and he fills a room; the energy in him vibrates and enlarges him. There's violence in him, even the dullest people can feel the passionate impulse, the threat of sudden action, the void of self-consciousness, the energy he carries around in him. Women change when he enters a room.

Solly entered the party to the sound of *Sergeant Pepper* and the girls changed. The gigglers giggled more infectiously, the sirens sang, the frosty ones offered their exquisite nonchalance. Anne drew in her breath and waited for him to see her and take her away.

And Isobel beside her didn't wait. She got up and walked toward him with the conscious dignity of a hero about to be awarded a medal, a prisoner about to be executed, a bride about to be married. While Anne held her breath and waited, Isobel moved and caught his eye.

He was wearing jeans and a filthy T-shirt and his hair was very black and thick and cut raggedly around his large head. His forearms made her soften, the way, later, a sleeping child would, or a sudden sunlit bank of moss. His eyes were unusual, not large but very dark, slashing his face in half horizontally. She said, 'My name is Isobel. I'll show you around.' And Michael laughed with what sounded like relief as he moved away from the door to let them through.

Once outside, she took fright and began to babble and walk very fast, scrambling along the trail to the dock, pointing out the boathouse, scurrying past cabins along beaten paths. She could feel him very close behind her and she moved faster still, aware of the darkness, the quiet, her own quick and shallow breaths and Solly very close, a large warmth behind her, a threat, a thrill. She clutched at her bare arms as she flitted back and forth. It was a hot night and she'd worn a tank top, not caring who saw her bony arms, like toothpicks, Michael said, because it was only Anne who had to look good. When she ran out of places to show him and things to say about them, she stopped short. 'That's all,' she said desperately. 'We've seen it all.' Anne was beautiful, smooth and clever and easy, and knew how to talk to boys.

'Where's your cabin?' he asked. He has the voice of someone who's forgotten to clear his throat. He can seduce a woman over the phone.

She turned and looked at him, her second look, just to make sure she'd been right the first time. Virginity was both an attractive ornament and a tiresome handicap. 'It's out on the point,' she said.

His hands came down on her bare shoulders. 'Look,' he whispered. 'I caught a firefly.'

Solly couldn't have told you why he picked up this little white girl. That's how he thought of her, although so far all his girls had been white; his upbringing had occurred in a sphere that was exclusively Anglo-Saxon, the exceptions being the sons of diplomats and dictators who were accorded an honorary whiteness. In his circle, however, the very best white was well toasted in summer and Isobel was underdone and thus an oddity.

When he entered the room, the faces that turned his way were the kind of faces he'd seen all his life. His sisters had these faces, so did his cousins; his early girlfriends had looked this way, plump and sure, smooth as boiled eggs. His last girlfriend had been a departure, a statement of protest if you like; skinny, demonic, unfashionably chic; she had worn short black leather skirts; people had stared; he'd liked that. It turned out, though, that she was afraid of his parents' silverware and had giggled and looked silly at dinner. Anne was next, just another girl of the type he understood, just another girl of the type that reassured his family.

His two older brothers went to the right parties and danced with the right girls and had the presence of mind to sow their wild oats where the weeds would do no harm. But Solly, the youngest, had cowed his family early on with a head-banging, shit-smearing babyhood. Born a skin too short, his mother would say with tired hope, when he burst into extravagant tears in public or bit the daughter of her closest friend. Later, he refused to ski, and played hockey instead of rugger and was banned from the club for not wearing whites. He was good at history but bad at math and said the stock market where his father worked was immoral. He got himself expelled from UCC so he could take shop at the public high school. He seduced his mother's friends and their daughters too and left them in tears.

He was convinced from an early age that he had been stolen, not from privilege by gypsies, but the reverse. How could he belong to these calm, chilly people, this quiet and stagnant caste? Somehow, he'd been mislaid by a bold, impassioned race. Somewhere, a man with battered hands, a woman with a swing in her hips and a rough tongue mourned his absence as they bickered over hot, fraught meals.

He knew from the start he was meant to be someone, a visionary, a purveyor of change, and change was precisely what his family feared. There was a connection through his mother to distillery money and distillery money meant rum-running not so long ago and distillery boys were expected to become doctors or missionaries or businessmen of impeccable practice: those few needed to work the business were careful philanthropists. Art, it was felt, might be permissible as a career within a generation or two; but for now art led to socialism, then to political dissent, protest, even to illegal activity, and then the family might have come full circle but without the profit. In another place it might have been a coup to count a smuggler among one's near ancestors but in Toronto wealth was expected to behave itself as if it had been silently and spotlessly acquired, as if God Himself had made a generous donation.

He didn't know the little white girl would stay forever. She was just someone new, someone different. There were so many women to be had and he could have them, he had discovered, for the asking.

Solly said, 'Come,' and Isobel went.

There was a place, he told her, on the far edge of the country where the stern, implacable land blurred with the sea, a place of mild winters and easy living, a soft, haunted place. Others were there: artisans and anarchists and beautiful dreamers. You could build a fine house out of driftwood, a fireplace out of river rock. You could pick your living off the beach. You could think for yourself and not for others. You could be free. It was the most beautiful place in the country. So Solly told her, his eyes on the horizon.

Isobel wasn't listening, not really. Solly said *come* and she went. There was no choice to be made, no option to be considered. It was a question of breathing or ceasing to breathe. She wanted to pry open his mouth and climb down his throat and curl up somewhere inside him. She wanted to roll herself out like the finest phyllo pastry and envelop his every contour. She had thought he would not say *come*, and then she thought she would die as simply and passively as a parasite plucked off its host.

Sometimes Isobel imagines that she has another self. The other was just a little more ambitious, a little more conservative; there was only a minuscule difference at the beginning. The other needed the extra two weeks' work at the shop. This girl turned down the invitation to the lake.

She quickly found the arty crowd at the university. She only attended the classes she thought worthwhile. She wasn't interested in art history or theory. She slung beer and pizza to put herself through school, never went home for the holidays, embraced narcissism as a requisite of artistic integrity, dyed her hair dead black, left school in a temper and lived the young artist's life of lavish penury – a cold, smelly room above a Chinese restaurant, alternately starving and eating out, going without electricity to buy $200 shoes.

She's middle-aged now, just like Isobel. She lives cheaply on an island somewhere. She keeps chickens, a noisy dog, a few casual, outdoor cats. She's begun to paint in oils again, but she's tried every medium. She's accepted as an artist in a modest Canadian way. It's possible to hear her name in certain circles, she's considered unspectacular but game, she's respected for having stuck to it so long; she has no money whatsoever. Every five years or so, she applies to the Canada Council and they remember her and send her a small grant, a kind of pension. She makes a meagre living breeding plants. She qualifies for a farm subsidy and raises Oriental poppies, a neglected species that has scope for the small hybridizer. She's trying to achieve a black; already her maroon is much sought after. She's well-known in the clubby, cozy gardening world. Sometimes she takes a wheel or two of slides and a sheaf of notes, gets on a ferry and gives a lecture to a plant society. She has a pricy list but there are always buyers. In June, people come to see her meadow where the poppies bloom white through ox-blood (and orange, of course; these she must rogue with fierce attention to their dogged roots.) She flags the pods to be saved for seed and, three weeks later, she sharpens her scythe and cuts the rest to the ground.

Men, and lately women, come and go. They stay for a year or two, never more, and she's glad of their company, though she's selfish and expects them to behave themselves and do as they're told. When they leave, she's content, only the food gets worse and the house is a wreck. She's known, in an ungossipy, subtextual way, for her lovers, but she's never been in love, except with herself. She never met Solly.

She's so light, so free of encumbrance, that she could float if she wanted to. She could take off. The poppies would survive. They're tough. The dogs and cats would eat the chickens. She could get on a ferry one day and never come back.

And Isobel, cramming clothes into her suitcase, terrified that Solly wouldn't bother to wait, did she once think of Anne, sobbing convulsively deep in the impeccable forest? She did not. She sliced Anne off like a ragged nail and tossed her away. She did it for love.

Frances called it an infatuation, a deprecating, unserious word, a word that implies superficiality and short-lived passion. Isobel, of course, called it love. She will never know now who was right, whether a few weeks of frenzied grief would have cured her of him. She knows that the sight of him at odd moments will still catch her breathless.

She thought he would not say *come*, and then she would die. But he said *come* and she went. And she lived.

The myth says they ran away – the children won't have it any other way – the sheer romance of it, the slap in the face of convention! – but there was nothing furtive about their departure. Having so easily lost its father, Isobel's family has always invested leave-takings with ceremony. They understand that the leaver may never come back.

They celebrate even the tiniest blips in their lives. As children, they all had a birthday party every year, even those years between their father and Marcel when the presents were Kleenex flowers and hand-me-down clothes. Even those months when Frances poured boiling water into the Nescafe jar to coax out the last cup of coffee and they ate salmon fishcakes three times a week. Even those birthdays when the children loudly resented the homemade cake because they couldn't afford the mix.

So when Solly said *come*, she had to take him home, so that they could be wished away properly, so that it would take. Isobel knew that she was just a whim, that soon another girl would walk toward him and catch his eye.

Frances had no choice but to let her go. She was, after all, on record as the theorist of the Progressive Imposition of Independence. For years she had proclaimed that the truly good and selfless mother must practise a gradual withdrawal of interest and affection from her child so that the child can leave without guilt. It was a theory that was much admired until it was found to be next to impossible in practice. Still, if Frances wished for apron strings, she couldn't and didn't show it.

She threw a party and everyone they knew came and inspected Solly with arms crossed and eyes narrowed and asked about his people and told him embarrassing stories about dirty diapers or cooking sherry and eventually got drunk and sentimental. It was just like a wedding and that's what Isobel has always considered it.

Photographs survive. Since this was merely a farewell party and not a wedding, there isn't one of Solly and Isobel together, unless you count a group shot taken by Bob which contains Isobel among others and a part of Solly's jeans.

The children enjoy this meagre evidence.

'That's Daddy's leg,' Suzannah will say to Monty.

'What happened to the rest of him?' Monty asks, aghast.

They moon over Isobel in a high-waisted white gauze dress, not really believing that their tough old mother was ever this young. Isobel looks about twelve and she now wonders how Frances could have stood for it.

Marcel slipped her two hundred dollars in case she changed her mind. Her mother had invited a lot of her acolytes and they huddled in a corner approving of Frances for letting Isobel live her own life and cursing Isobel for screwing it up.

They all ate and drank too much and fell asleep in unnatural positions and were bitchy the next morning because Frances made them get up early to see Solly and Isobel off.

Rex coughed and roared. Solly pulled out, and Isobel turned and watched her mother grow smaller and smaller.

Chapter Six

It was just as well they never made it to Florencia Bay. A few years later, the colony that Solly had heard about was broken up and moved along. A national park was to be made, and a few magnificent modern totems and a bunch of hippie huts didn't represent a culture venerable enough to be preserved. But even if the commune had survived, Long Beach would never have satisfied Isobel and Solly. They had thought about it too much, raised the shanties and the totems in their minds, carved and coloured them, felt the pull of the sea around their legs, heard voices in the wind and found neighbours as pure and kind as angels.

They never even saw it. Solly refused to go; it would be a mournful place, he said. Now again, it's the place to go, worth the hideous, jostling, trailer-ridden drive to admire the whales and protect the old growth, or to surf the icy waves that break for miles along the beach.

But Long Beach was their purpose and once the journey had a purpose, then its length and path didn't matter. If there was money for gas and the landscape said nothing to them, they'd drive for two days running, Solly's old Ford basting the hem of the country. When there wasn't money for gas or food or beer or grass or second-hand paperbacks, they'd stop and work at whatever they could find, the more menial and boring the better because the journey was what mattered. Sometimes a valley would reach out to them on the Trans-Canada or a hitchhiker would tell a tale of a compelling place, or a name – Utah – would resound in their ears. They were drawn to names. They stayed in Thunder Bay until they heard the thunder. They zipped up to Head-Smashed-In just to eat ice cream. Time they had to squander with extravagance.

They owned time and a car and nothing else. They had Solly's '63 Ford Fairlane, Rex. Rex was pale blue and had the heavy passiveness of a plough horse. Rex liked downhills the best. Something loose in the fit of the windows went WHEEEEEE on the downhills. Something under the floorboards went UNGH going up.

Isobel takes that trip out and polishes it sometimes. They might, like others they met on the road, never have stopped travelling; they might have worked their way around and around in spirals on the globe, always another spot unvisited, another sight unseen. All that is needed is that the travelling time seem to have no end. There has to be no return ticket, no job on the 15th, no days to be counted, no end in sight. Isobel and Solly knew, they thought, where they were going, but they were not expected there. They could spend the rest of their lives getting there if that was what they wanted. The rest of their lives was enormous.

Later, when other travellers wandered into the Farm, they put them to work at dull, heavy jobs that required no training or commitment and woke up each morning expecting them to be gone.

Even now when good, responsible, pay-the-mortgage jobs are hard to find, the footloose can pick up money. There are always dirty dishes, unpicked crops, beer to be slung and trees to be planted. There's money for gas and food and fun, road money. And when the need to run is fierce, there's a young body to be rented out, a purse to be snatched, a pill to be peddled. Some of these kids wander into the Project. They've heard about it at their squat or on the street but Solly no longer remembers the pull of the horizon and only if they've lost the vague unfocused look of wanderlust are they allowed to stay.

'Are you a zealot?' Terry McKenna asked, not long ago.

'Fuckin' right,' Solly snarled.

'Mrs Whitechapel, also known as Isobel Lamb, who has eight

natural children ...' Is she imagining things or is there just the slightest emphasis on the number eight? To have eight children is unnatural as we all know, the moderator seems to say. The establishment press have decided that if they wrap the story in a thick enough layer of thoughtful analysis they can pick it up without soiling their hands. Now a member of the panel, some kind of psychologist, talks about compulsive behaviour and martyr complexes, the kind of personality that would feel compelled to produce eight children. Someone else mentions a couple who has adopted and fostered more than fifty kids. There is a strong suggestion that this much good-doing is more than a little bit sick.

Dirt broke the story. *Dirt* is anything but establishment press. Isobel had never heard of *Dirt*. *Dirt* is powerful, though. Marnie knew. It was Marnie who told her what time to watch so she could creep downstairs and turn it on at whisper volume and sample its cotton-candy revelation.

Solly becomes deaf the instant *Dirt* is mentioned. He thinks *Dirt* is beneath contempt. He will never forgive her for what she's about to do.

On TV, the young man looks real enough but viewed in person, readied for the camera with moulded hair and orange skin and highlighted features, he's clearly made of plastic.

Isobel has allowed herself to be made up too. They've insisted on it. They've said trust us: if you go on without makeup, you'll look washed out, distraught.

'But I am distraught. That's why I'm here.'

They pat her hand and speak in murmurs: distraught people are not uncommon in the studio. 'But if you don't look right, the viewers won't like you. You won't deserve their empathy. You're a striking woman. You have to look like they wish they looked for them to empathize. Empathy's what we're after, isn't it? You need the viewers' help. You need the coffee shop waitress in Ames who served Magnolia yesterday. She looks at you, she sees someone just like her, only better. She calls in.'

So Isobel sits on an ill-balanced chair with her face thickly painted and her hair twice as big as it should be. What if Maggie doesn't recognize her? What if she catches a glimpse of her on some barroom TV and fails to recognize her own mother?

'Are you ready to try a take?' the plastic man asks. 'Just remember, the angle's Magnolia. Not that you're not a fascinating person yourself. I'm sure you are.'

'No. I'm not fascinating. Can I smoke?'

'Not on camera. It would make you unsympathetic to our viewers. I think we've agreed that we need them on our side.'

Who the hell are these people anyway? Millions and millions of people watch *Dirt* every night, so she's told, and some of them smoke like chimneys, she's sure.

'We'll start with me. I'll give them the background and then we'll play the tape from last week when the story broke, and then the interview with the Mountie. It's a darned shame about the uniform. I thought they always wore red. Then a clip of Magnolia's latest video and then you. Keep it simple.'

Isobel is going to cry and ruin the mask of make-up. And who will comfort her? Not this cool, competent mob, who are only interested in packaging her for sale.

The young man leans forward and speaks confidingly to his camera. Isobel has her own camera watching her. She's heard that it looks like an eye, but that's a lie. An eye has intelligence. An eye reacts. This looks more like a vast and indiscriminate black hole that will gobble her up because she's in its way.

Now it's Isobel's turn. She peers into the black hole and says, 'Magnolia, please come home. We love …' and then she breaks down, and tears and mucus gush in an unadmirable manner and the plastic man is absolutely delighted.

Discovery, exposure, notoriety; life continues in spite of disaster. Isobel should know this. People must eat, go to school, wear clean socks, be driven to soccer games and music lessons, wash, breathe.

It's mid-afternoon and they've just picked up Toby from kindergarten. Kindergarten terrifies Toby, but he understands that he's five now and that kindergarten is expected of five so he goes and teeters on the trembly edge of control for two and a half hours every morning. Isobel likes to be there when the classroom door is thrown open so that he can see her right away.

They've barged through the reporters, faces set, shoulders straight, eyes down. Isobel is getting good at it. At first, she said 'please' and 'excuse me' until Marnie warned her not to. *On TV, courtesy comes across as apology. You might as well admit you're guilty.*

And notice how they stand right in your way. You're not exactly going to head-butt them, they know that. But you've got to blow right through them. This is like a new skill you've got to learn. You're kind of a star now. You've got to consider your image.

Now Toby is happily comparing the exact volume of apple juice in his cup to Monty's and checking his oatmeal cookies for things.

Winnie comes home while Isobel is peeling carrots for the stew. She sniffs audibly, wrinkles up her face and stares in shock at her mother as if she's caught her frying up puppies. 'And just what am I supposed to eat while the rest of you stuff yourselves with dead animals?'

'We had tofu casserole last night and I had to watch everybody pick around it and red beans and rice the night before and most people,' she's beginning to bellow, 'and most people in this family are not vegetarian!'

Winnie grabs one of the carrots from the cutting board and inspects it minutely for blood. 'You know, it's the meat that makes you so aggressive,' she says in her best mild and reasonable voice. She wanders off munching, soon to collapse in a misunderstood heap on her bed. Winnie is thirteen.

Isobel feels awful and yells down the stairs, 'I'll make you cheese on toast, okay?' She stands there listening while the wooden spoon drips stew juice on the carpet. 'Is that okay?' she shrieks. Now the pure and lonely call of Winnie's flute floats up the stairs. And Isobel doesn't understand flute.

'Oh boy, meat,' Mick says, dumping his books, his backpack and his soccer cleats on the kitchen table.

'I love you, Micky.'

'Hi, Mick,' Toby says.

'Hi, Mick,' Monty says. Mick took them to the park twice and sometimes wrestles with them during the first intermission.

'Yeah. Okay. So. I need two seventy-five and three twenty-five for tomorrow and you have to sign these,' he says ponderously, hauling two crumpled papers out of his back pocket. Then he picks up an oatmeal cookie and starts checking it for things.

Marnie clumps up the back steps from the studio and cuffs Mick on the top of the head as she passes him to wash her hands at the sink. Mick tells her to piss off and she produces a horrified moue, and Isobel, slicing onions now, is obliged to groan and make a face while the little boys mouth *piss off* at each other with rapt faces. The kids spew expletives with the sudden brutality of hail. Solly swears casually and with relish and opposes all forms of censorship, which doesn't help. Isobel has composed a short speech about the tailoring of language to situation and the power of expletives used sparingly, like condiments. 'Like chili peppers,' she always says.

Marnie winks at the little boys, thrusts her hands into the flour bin, then gently hip-checks Isobel out of the way so she can open the oven door and take out the enormous beige bowl in which she always sets her bread dough to rise. Marnie bakes six loaves of beautiful bread every second day.

Solly found Marnie in Gastown. In the old days, he trolled for these kids in boarded-up buildings and seedy hotels on Granville or in the Downtown East Side. He's stopped lately, but the kids still come. There's always a little gang sleeping in the garage on bunks built by the first little gang nearly twenty years ago. Some, like Marnie, come hurt and searching directly off the streets, hard, hooked, bleeding, even dying. Some come wearing black and equipped with jargon from the Emily Carr School of Art. Some come from dingy rooms full of family over corner stores. Some come from houses with tennis courts and portes cochères and pay for the privilege. The ones who are scary are told to go away; the hungry are fed; the sick are taken to the family doctor whose nurse pretends not to notice that the kid and the health care card don't match. (*God only knows what my health record looks like,* Willow said, taking her card from her mother. *It's not like the old days, Mum. It's all on computer. We probably all have AIDS, according to the government. Besides, there's such a thing as abuse of the system, you know.*)

They can claim a few successes. One of the native kids is carving for David Linley in London. Another is the accounts manager at IKEA. Isobel and Solly believe they've done good but they can't prove it. It isn't easy doing good; it's just as hard as doing evil; only doing nothing is easy. Some of the street kids resent them, sneer at the two-wheelers and the braces and the seat belts and the regular meals. They become obnoxious, even violent. Others sink into the Project like a feather bed and do nothing but smoke and gossip and turn up for meals. Solly and Isobel learned from the Farm that you can't commit wholesale charity without inviting disaster. They learned to be ruthless. Kids are analysed and rejected for their ability to respond to the good done to them. Efficiency has crept in.

Sometimes the rich kids bring pitas or smoked salmon or pizza. Sometimes the poor kids do too and everyone eats as fast as they can to destroy the evidence. Isobel and Marnie make every meal for sixteen and have saucepans the size of occasional tables.

Now Solly is saying they can't afford the Project any more, that its time is past. He talks to bankers these days. He meets with real estate agents. He becomes more ordinary every day.

Isobel puts the stew on high and, as she turns away from the stove, over Monty's curly black head, she sees, she thinks,

Auntie Win standing in the unlit hall. A glimpse in peripheral vision; when she actually looks, there's nothing there. Monty turns around and stares.

Isobel sits down quickly, pours tea and lights a cigarette. Marnie disapproves of smoking, never drinks coffee or alcohol and doesn't really condone tea. She likes her tea as pale as old photographs and heavily disguised with milk and sugar.

'Marnie, have you noticed anything funny about the house lately?'

Marnie clears her throat. 'If you mean that smell in the downstairs hall, I've been meaning to talk to you about it. I'm pretty sure it's some kind of mould. Somebody's gonna have to take up that floor pretty soon. And I got a flea bite the other day. We'll have to buy oranges again.'

Ordinarily, Isobel is galvanized by a flea bite. She's convinced the household is only one step away from utter squalor. She's always running into somebody's mother in the checkout line at Pharmasave. Somebody's mother has combed her hair and is buying something commendable like toothpaste and can't help but notice that Isobel has need of flea powder, pinworm medication or lice shampoo.

'Nothing? Nothing at all? Nothing even a little strange?' she asks again.

'You know you really shouldn't smoke around the kids. I've told you that,' Marnie says firmly. For a minute, Isobel thinks she's suggesting that cigarettes are hallucinogenic. 'Don't you ever watch TV?' Marnie watches a lot of TV out in the garage. She favours pseudo-documentaries on mysterious phenomena, or dramatized life stories in which awful things happen to innocent people. She mistakes reality for truth. 'I like facts,' she explains. And this is clear even in the kitchen, which she treats like a chemistry lab, sifting dry ingredients, leveling off when measuring, worrying about pinches and dashes because they can't be quantified.

Marnie likes to bake. When she bakes, she smiles and hums

along to alternative radio and the little ones sit at the kitchen table and eat grubby scraps of pastry. She spends most of her money in kitchen shops where she buys only the best: thick white custard cups, heavy black cookie sheets, pretty enamel colanders, knives as small as emery boards and as big as chain saws.

Isobel stubs out her cigarette. 'I just wondered.' She doesn't want to use a suggestive word, like 'ghost' or 'haunt' to Marnie. Marnie likes facts. But Monty is still staring.

'What did you see, sweetheart?'

'Nothing,' he says. ''Nother cookie, Marn?'

'You've had enough.' Marnie says. 'Don't you think you should turn down that stew?'

Marnie is slipping into servanthood and Isobel is letting her do it. As Marnie says, she was lousy at furniture anyway and was still sanding after six months. Solly makes every new kid sand by hand for the first three months. Sanding is tedious and exhausting. Three months of sanding represents a sincere commitment to the Project.

Marnie opens the door of the broom closet and nothing falls out. Marnie has tidied it. She finds the Comet and Lysol and slouches off in search of a bathroom.

Only two weeks ago, a neighbour came over and said she'd had it up to here with Molly Maid: 'Maybe you could send over one of your girls,' she suggested, smiling and charitable. 'I'd like to help out.'

'They're apprentice cabinet makers,' Isobel snapped, 'not cleaning ladies.' Except Marnie. But the fact remains that Marnie knows to pick up and hug a toddler who's purple with fury, Marnie has the guts to remove splinters and swab grit out of scrapes, Marnie is willing to wash hair and wipe bums. She's impervious to manipulation and doesn't believe in corporal punishment, junk food or God. What would Isobel do if she left? When Isobel did it alone, the house was never tidy, never clean, never organized. Germs flourished, assignments were lost, the school's hamster took a suicide leap off a top bunk and had to be given a humiliating playground funeral. People assume that a woman with nine children has a system. They imagine charts and timetables and lots of lists and clothing colour-coded by size and everybody pitching in with jolly attitudes. A mother of two will say to Isobel, 'How do you cope? I'm barely coping with two.' And Isobel will answer 'I'm barely coping with nine.' It seems the state of barely coping stretches to meet the need. Isobel cleans in frantic, last-minute bursts while Marnie vacuums refrigerator coils, scrubs fingerprints off woodwork and gouges out the crud between the bathroom tiles. Marnie knows the purpose of every attachment that comes with the vacuum cleaner. If Isobel takes Marnie shopping, she's there to say, 'What about shampoo?' or 'Nobody liked those crackers the last time we bought them.'

But is this doing good, plucking a kid off the street and using her as a servant? It sure doesn't look good. And people are watching now. What a few weeks ago was a charmingly eccentric household is now suspect. The Neighbourhood has called the zoning department. The rich kids are being hauled away and put into sailing school instead.

Marnie is unimpressed by the fuss and shoulders her way through the reporters. She thinks Magnolia is a spoiled brat.

She sticks her head around the door. 'You're supposed to call the doctor, remember? And that tap's dripping still. I thought someone was going to fix it. I can try if you want. Oh, and we're almost out of toilet paper again.'

What Isobel wants, not exactly more than anything in the world, not more than having Magnolia back, not more than peace, health, love, but more than, say, a microwave oven or a second car, is a large closet in each of the two bathrooms, a closet big enough to hold stacks and stacks of toilet paper so that she can get Safeway to deliver it once a year in one of their trucks and they will never, ever run out.

Chapter Seven

The Spanish sailors were dancing on deck when it was sighted, so they named the little island Las Danzas and sailed on. A few years later, it was found all over again by the British who would have followed their stolid tradition and called it after a monarch, a home town or a worthy shipmate if not for the cartographer who knew of the Spanish name. Las Danzas was entirely too Spanish and would never do for this disputed land, but the skipper had a taste for romance and it was called Lost Answers Island before they too sailed away and the native people pulled their canoes out of hiding and went on calling it what they had called it for a thousand years.

Lost Answers Island.

They went for the name.

The nearer Solly and Isobel got to Long Beach, the more they began to fear its approaching solid thump. It was famous in its way among people on the move. In Kingston, it was paradise: no winter and brotherly love. In Winnipeg, it was no winter and great rolling breakers as far as the eye could see; the edge of the country, precarious, magnetic. By Calgary, where even the hippies were shrewd and practical, they began to hear about the rain and the wind. In Vancouver, where rain was unremarkable, the wind became deafening; passions and jealousy reigned at the colony; a shack had been burnt down, they said, over a woman. A red-headed girl who called herself Singing Cloud said she had barely escaped with her sanity. She said people had begun to hear voices in the wind. She said people had begun to walk into the breakers, which were, she said, like liquid ice. The man who carved the totem poles had disappeared into the rainforest. The wind kicks up the sand, she said. It scours your skin. The beach is so huge, she said, so blurred by mist, that you can never be sure it's still there. The storms come up, she said, and the great logs move and crash and talk in splintered voices.

So they slowed to a shuffle and when Rex wouldn't start they took the chance to make the journey longer still. With the help of a crew who had seen it all before, they pushed the car off the ferry deck and left it by the side of the road and hitched a ride on top of a cord of wood in the back of a pickup truck.

It was Saturday morning and Saturday was market day at Lost Answers. People came into town to sell, to buy, to trade, to gossip, to catch the fine expansive light of Indian summer before marketing became a chilly, scurrying chore. The market had an impromptu and haphazard look about it. Vendors traded from lawn chairs and TV trays, cardboard boxes, crates and bridge tables. Potters hovered nervously over displays of speckled brown earthenware. A silversmith guarded a case of jewellery next to a tired old man hunched over three pumpkins, a bunch of dahlias and a dozen rusty, swollen paperback books. A woman in scarves offered herb sprigs rooted in egg cartons. There was stained glass and a lot of macramé of questionable purpose. Girls with faces as fresh as pansies thrust out samples of oily hummus on whole-grain bread. There were apples free of pesticides but not of pests, Indian muslin clothing in the colours of precious jewels, chipped bits of china and handknit layette sets. People offered hens for honey, firewood for stereo equipment, raspberry canes for potatoes.

Isobel spotted a little girl who was trying to subdue a simmering blanket contained in a basket. 'Stop that!' she kept saying as she slapped down one corner of the blanket after the other.

'What's in the basket?'

The little girl dragged it toward Isobel. 'Have a look,' she offered glumly.

The basket contained three kittens: one black, one orange and one tortoise shell. The kittens blinked in the sunlight and studied life outside the basket with quivering vigilance.

'Izzy,' Solly began.

'Are they for free?'

'Yeah. You can pick one if you like,' the little girl allowed, as if the offer had been wrung from her under torture. Someone had decided to let her bangs grow out and they were not very successfully held back by yellow barrettes.

'Isobel, we can't take a cat on the road. You know that. We'd lose it.'

She looked up at Solly, squinting in the foreign white light, so unlike the yellow light that illuminates the country they had just crossed. Perhaps they were in Greece or Madagascar.

'We're nearly there,' she said.

'A cat is a responsibility.'

She laughed at his pomposity. 'Yes, Daddy.'

He didn't like that and turned away.

'I really like marmalade cats,' she began, and watched as the little face solidified with fear. 'But I think on the whole that tortoiseshells are my favorite.' She hauled out a kitten which went spread-eagled with panic.

The little girl relaxed. 'Oh sure.' she said, shoving the orange one securely under the blanket again. 'Sure. Maybe you like black ones too? There were six altogether and Dad said if I got rid of five, I could keep the last one. But he said to push the girl cats cause boys are less trouble. I don't know why.'

Isobel upended the squeaking kitten and peered under its tail. 'This area looks kind of ambiguous to me,' she said to Solly. 'What do you think?'

'It's a female. I can tell by the squawk.'

'That one's a girl. I guess you don't need the black one too?' the little girl asked.

'No, we don't,' Solly said firmly, watching as Isobel disentangled the kitten from the neck of her T-shirt.

'What should we call it?' she asked him as they walked away. 'Albatross,' he muttered. She was losing him. He would leave her here.

They'd eaten the last of their money in the form of ferryboat chowder and they had to find work, but the word among the stall-keepers was that no one was hiring. The tourist season was over. The growing season was over. Nobody much worked in the winter anyway. In the end, they sat down beside an old woman selling apples and began to rummage through their backpacks looking for something to trade. They weren't worried. The island was full of fields and forests and the tent was small and green and not very noticeable and would do no harm. They would earn money somehow. They always had. And they were young and beautiful, and hope and good feeling shone out of their eyes. That was then.

'He wants to put me in one of them places,' the old apple lady announced to nobody in particular. Solly and Isobel pretended not to hear as people do when met with gentle madness. 'Says he can't live with himself otherwise. Says he'll take care of the money side of things. Big shot! But I told him I have sworn a solemn oath to die out here in the real world.' Here, she laid a hand on her heart like an actor and turned toward them and it was listen or leave. They had nowhere to go. They listened.

'You ever looked into the eyes of the old folks in a home? Home, they call it. Hah! My sister-in-law, they put her there after she broke her hip. I'd go to visit her on a Sunday, bring her some cookies and a bunch of good garden flowers, not the store kind that look too good to be true for an hour and then wilt. She liked the cookies, had a real sweet tooth at the end. Well, so do I, I guess. My old granny went the same way, ate nothing but sugary things before she died. Used to drive my mother crazy.' Here she felt able to take her eyes off them long enough to offer them the last two apples from the table in front of her. Solly stretched out to accept them. Food was not to be refused.

'Anyway, my sister-in-law, Emily she was called, she'd be waiting for me all set up in the lounge in a wheelchair with her hair combed like she never combed it once in her life. And she had *pretty* hair, too. Nice and thick. And I thought, This isn't so bad, at least she's got her lipstick on, she hasn't given up on life. 'Cause I don't care what you girls today think, a woman without lipstick is having trouble in her mind. That lipstick was just as pink as cotton candy, not her shade, but still, I thought, a good sign, and then I looked at all the other old ladies, and their mouths were all that same candy pink, like the nurses had lined them up after lunch and slapped it on, just like painting a fence. And her eyes, my chickens, her eyes would make you cry. I got so I couldn't look into them. No way I could take a crippled woman home with me, not even if she had put up with my own brother for forty years, which I can tell you, was no fun at all. So I just prattled on, the way you do, local gossip, how much we'd made at the church bazaar and guess who had to get married. It got so before I left the farm, I'd take an envelope and write down a list of topics, so there'd never be a lull, you know? Just in case she burst out and begged me to take her home. Just in case she started to cry. But she never did. She wasn't mean like me, I guess. She always put up with things. She was never one to make a fuss. Well, she died anyway. I guess that's just the way. Life's a misery near the end so you won't miss it that much when you go.'

She sighed and began to pack up her things. 'You don't have a car by any chance? Maybe heading out toward McKenzie Point?'

'We do ...' Isobel began.

'Unless you mean one that works,' Solly finished.

'Oh, well. Never mind. My neighbour brought me in, you see, but he's long gone. I never learned to drive, don't really know why, now. I think I'll just pop over to the Red&White for a pound of coffee and head on home.'

She was a hugely fat woman, as solid and white as a snowman and she wheezed as she stood up and folded the lawn chair that had miraculously contained her.

Solly stood up too. 'We can't give you a ride,' he said, 'but we can escort you. You've got a lot to carry there.' He picked up the apple crate and handed the chair to Isobel. Solly would help this old woman without expectation of repayment, but gallantry, he had found, often paid. Even the most angular and forbidding of women became motherly around him. Matrons and barmaids and tough old tobacco farm wives slipped him sandwiches and cookies. They changed sheets in guest rooms for Solly.

They got a ride with a carpenter who knew Mrs Ferguson well enough to call her Ma and whose eyes flicked over Isobel and Solly like searchlights.

She lived in a silver trailer in what had once been a garden. The path of long wet squashed grass was edged with white painted rocks, and a rugosa rose the size of a room bristled with thorns, its small magenta flowers clashing with the orange of its hips.

'Just put that crate down around back. I'll give you coffee,' Mrs Ferguson said, groaning up the steps and pulling open the door, which shrieked like a parrot. 'Now, darn it all, I forgot the milk again. I hope you don't favour milk.'

The trailer smelled of apples and cats and something warm and tangy which might have been old woman's body. The cats came forward to investigate the kitten, decided it was not worth knowing and went out with tails held high. There was no room for three people unless one was in the toilet and another crouched on a shelf, but they managed by clearing the bed of at least a bushel of apples to knock it around and tuck away cushions until it became a table. 'Everything in here is at least one other thing, except me and the cats, that is,' Mrs Ferguson said proudly. She seemed to have forgotten that there was no milk because she opened the fridge and peered into it. There was little to peer at beyond many more apples and a double file of eggs. The window above the table that was also a bed looked out back onto the grid of an orchard. Beneath the trees, brown hens scratched and bickered in the long, tired grass.

Mrs Ferguson wedged herself in between the bench and the table. She drank her coffee from a mug made of heavy white plastic with Phil's Auto Body printed on the side, its inside the colour of bad teeth; but she poured theirs into cups and saucers of thinnest cream and pale green Belleek with handles as fine and graceful as calligraphy.

She was afraid that there were no cookies, 'though I could fry you up a coupla eggs.' She poked Solly, 'You look all right, but your girl here's too scrawny. Well, this is a treat. I don't get too many friends coming by. Mind you, most of them are dead and I'm not sure I'd want to see them. The Reverend Father, he's a well-meaning man, for all he lets them play the guitar at services. Why God would want to listen to guitar music, I'm sure I couldn't say. He usually comes the last Tuesday of the month, and he won't turn down an egg. And there's the woman from the hospital, she comes every second Monday but all she wants to do is clean. Course, soon as I get around to making it, there'll be applesauce cake. I been looking forward to apple- sauce cake. Bought some flour especially for it. Can't waste the apples.'

'What about your family?' Solly asked.

'Ferguson and me, we just had the one boy. I couldn't seem to hold on to the babies after that. Miscarried three times. And our boy, Dean, he's in Calgary now. Handles people's money, you know. Not exactly a banker, in fact he looked pretty put out when I called him that. He wasn't interested in the land like his dad was. Didn't want the farm. And you can't make people unhappy just to please you.' She shot them a shrewd look. 'I don't want you to get the wrong idea. Dean's a good man. He's got four kids, two of them at the university and a sweet wife. She writes once a month and, just between you and me, I get the feeling handling money but not being a banker isn't just the right line of work to be in right now.

'They wanted me to move in with them in Calgary but I just

can't stomach that place in winter. I tried it for eight whole months, and I tell you the snow melts and everything's beige underneath, like something that hasn't been cooked long enough. And I like to go outside, you see. They keep talking about the sunshine, and fine, it's sunny, but unless you wrap up every last piece of you, it'll freeze and fall off. Anyway, Dean just got so het up about me living in the old place, afraid I'd fall down the stairs or something. Then we had that fight about the home. He sent for their brochure, you see, and it looks pretty good on paper, but I guess I told you about that. So this is what you call a compromise. No upkeep in a trailer. He worries about upkeep. No stairs neither and the mailman comes by every day. So I get to live on the road corner and he gets to sleep nights.'

She fell silent and seemed to forget they were there. Solly eased his shoulders and breathed shallowly; he felt too big for the wizened space, but Isobel was fascinated by its clever compaction, the magic of the table that was also a bed, the sink that could be a counter, the tiny bathroom, the Barbie fridge. They drank their coffee slowly and waited for the next thing to happen.

Mrs Ferguson slipped gently from wakefulness into sleep, wedged upright in the banquette, her head nodding against the trailer window, her hands still clasped around her coffee mug. The kitten had found a wooden bowl on top of the fridge and had curled up there. The very young and the very old slept without guilt and the trailer was silent except for the plink of hesitant rain on its metal roof.

'Let's have a look at this old place,' Solly whispered. Come. Stay. Turn this way. A smile in his eyes, a whisper so low it was nearly inaudible, a suggestion so intimate you had to be as close as his skin, his warm hand on the cold inside of her arm. So it was.

Isobel found a tartan blanket and wrapped it around the old lady.

'We should take the packs,' he whispered again. 'You never

know, do you, Izzy? You have to be ready for anything.'

'She didn't say we could use it,' a protest as flimsy as airmail paper. She was going and he knew it.

'We probably won't be able to. It's probably burned down or collapsed. We're only looking. We're curious, that's all. We won't hurt it. You know that.'

'What about the kitten?'

'We'll be back for the kitten.'

The farm gate was at the next turning. Stone pillars boasted of grandeur, but the drive itself was cramped and overgrown; the woods were closing in on it like thick green syrup. It was second-growth, Solly said, pointing out ludicrously big stumps lopped off head high but still not utterly dead, making planters for moss and opportunistic shrubs. Impossible to accept that this land had been scraped clean within the century, that the cedars which stretched out of sight were still in their gangly youth. The forest floor was laid with tripcords of native black-berry and billowed thigh-high in a tangle of sword ferns and evergreen shrubs they would eventually identify as salal and Oregon grape. Later, Isobel would gather posies of vanilla leaf to scent the house over winter. They would hack paths through the woods, lift moss to uncover oyster mushrooms, gather kin-dling sticks and the flaking cinnamon bark of arbutus. Later, they would own this woods and not fear it, but now it was for-eign and they kept to the narrow driveway and the birds broke off their gossip until they were safely past. It was October now, and at home the woods would be in flames ready to die down bare and open to view, but this forest was evergreen and intended to keep its secrets.

Where the green watery light became yellow, the road remembered itself, stopped deferring to the old stumps and ran straight and serious through the neglected fields to the farm.

Solly lifted his head and took in at once the house, the barn, the sheds, the fields, the fences, the orchard, the broad border of sombre forest, and saw a life of fixing and building and making and growing, heard women in the kitchen and sheep in the field and industry in the barn. He saw the fields and fence posts but not the tussocks of meadow grass left too long uncut, the invading force of broom and nettle and wild rose. (Isobel would strike hardwood cuttings from the roses and plant a hedge beside the vegetable garden and would make a mistake in cooking the hips and they'd all get itchy bum.)

Solly saw what he could make of the place.

Isobel saw the prosperous farmer with his acres of timber cleared back to allow a wide well of white light at ground level, the makeshift old cabin donated to the chickens, the proud erection of this grand new house, his boast, built from a book of designs sent over from Victoria, the wife's selection. The pretty daughters, the fine, strong sons lined up on the porch, as full of promise as the orchard trees which had just begun to bear.

Gables, a turret, gingerbread, a fine front porch. *We are rich and comfortable here, we have a porch to sit on and the time to use it. We are landowners, gentry, never mind what we left behind, the wretched hopelessness of it, never mind the fear and hardship of those first years, of freezing and starving and hitching ploughs to each other, of days spent felling trees that held up the sky and kept the sun from our faces and the rain from our crops, that shook the world when they fell and made wood enough to build a mansion. We have worked like slaves and nature has given us riches, fine timber and fresh soil and clean water and sunshine and rain in their seasons.*

Never mind that we are bent and old. We have this farm, this gentleman's house to show for our lives. Our sons have shoes, our daughters stockings. Remember that we started with nothing and this farm is what we made, this good strong house that will keep our family for generations. How could that proud pioneer know that within the century his fine house would stand empty and what was left of his dynasty would reside in a silver trailer down the road?

'Well, stupid old Dean,' Solly said. 'Can you believe it? I bet he's got a split level in Calgary.'

'With two and a half bathrooms.'

'Yup. Those bathrooms say it all, don't they?'

They pried up a window. Solly walked around banging walls and stamping on floorboards, pointing out the extravagant Victorian dimensions. A front room, a back room, the two connected by pocket doors which had come off their runners and screamed when they tried to slide them. Two fireplaces, an enormous inefficient kitchen with a wood-range and no cupboards. A cold room off the earthen basement. Up the broad stairs to four bedrooms and up narrow stairs to three more. A bathroom as big as a parlour. An outhouse at the end of the back path, a chicken coop, an old barn full of feral cats, a tool-shed full of tools and mice, sheds small and numerous and of unguessable purpose, the ground rough and lumpy with unmown grass. They explored like children in an adventure story, back into the house, which was cold and damp to the timbers. Isobel shivered and heard the house beg for the lighting of fires.

'Can you hear it?' she asked.

'Yup,' Solly said, pulling her down on the kitchen floor, lifting her skirt. 'Yup, I hear it. It's saying stay.' She felt it as he brushed his lips against her inner thigh; she heard it in the breathing of the floorboards, that the farm was built to be full and busy with baled hay and mended fences and fires chasing the damp up the chimney to the outside where it belonged. Men were meant to have calloused hands and women to have babies. Corners were meant to be swept and furniture polished and washing was meant to hang on the line. Loving possession was ownership.

They made love and Willow began on the cold speckled linoleum. And what did the Farm say as they slipped and slid, moaned and sighed, as they did what the farmer and his wife had done only after dark under scratchy wool blankets and in silence lest they offend God? Isobel would always hear the past at the Farm. The wisps of memory that wafted like dust balls down corridors, the threads of thought trapped in corners, the howls in the chimney told her that their style was an affront but their company was welcome. It was meant, she told Solly. We were meant to be here.

She felt nothing like that when she came to the Vancouver house, but then it was just a hiding place, a bolt-hole, and they were running away from the Farm and were not in a position to choose.

They slept wrapped in curtains in the biggest bedroom, had blackberries for breakfast and walked back with owner's eyes to be charming to Mrs Ferguson.

Well, she was charmed. Neighbours again and young, juicy ones. Able to prune the apples once she taught them how. Likely to drop by unexpectedly like beams of winter sunlight, full of energy and promise, bringing bread and salad greens and the first month's rent, not much but better than nothing. The old cookstove glimmering with heat. Of course she was charmed.

When Dean called, she found her maternal voice and armed it with rental income and general maintenance and the possibility of a stroke or a broken hip.

'Hippies!' Dean was aghast. 'What if they take it into their heads to murder you in your bed, Mother?'

'For what?' she cackled. 'They've already got what they want from me. They're not the trailer type. They're more romantic than the likes of us.'

'People like that don't need a reason, Mother. They're like as not crazed on drugs. Maybe satanists.'

'Dean, I keep telling you. I'm old and I know you feel bad about that, but I still got most of my marbles. You think I don't know nice kids when I see them? Who was the first to say Wes Connell's boy would go to the bad? Me, that's who, and before he was out of grade school. I can tell smart from stupid and good from bad and lazy from go-get-'em just as well as I always could and you better believe it. That is, unless you're planning to move back here and run the farm anytime soon.' This was her trump card.

She put the phone down with a clatter that made the trailer ring and smiled broadly at Solly.

So the Farm dropped into their hands like a fallen leaf or bird-shit, unexpected and dubious of value but free for the having. And Isobel saw Solly stop watching the horizon and look instead at his feet and the ground beneath them. He joined the library and took out books on poultry management and organic gardening and woodworking. He traded Rex for an old pick-up truck. He drove into town and stood around in front of the general store with other men in coveralls and gum boots. Pretty soon, there were chickens and a big vegetable garden all deer-fenced and the porch steps fixed and the grass mown and the road cleared back and the chimneys swept. Isobel scrubbed the outhouse and limed it and polished the stove and learned its quirks and turned chicken manure into the garden and made nettle soup and picked bucket after bucket of blackberries and late apples and made pies and crisps and sauce and chutney and cobbler and sold it by the slice at the market to people who had more than enough blackberries of their own. We'll never get scurvy, Solly said.

The proud old house couldn't look anything but shabby; it was too large and expensive an undertaking to paint it and they only patched the roof. If anything, they deliberately avoided the appearance of respectability. They laughed at new cars and white picket fences and the Sears catalogue. They thought they were perfect.

And in her snug silver trailer just up the road, Mrs Ferguson talked to her cats and felt less alone than before.

Chapter Eight

They began with what they had: mushrooms, apples, rosehips and blackberries, seven bedrooms, a deep well, a woodlot and a shedful of old tools. It didn't occur to them that what they had belonged, in fact, to Ma Ferguson. When Isobel found three boxes of canning jars in the cellar, she boiled them up to fill with apple chutney without a second thought. The apples would only fall and rot and sustain the wasps. But for her, the jars would stay empty until they grew so brittle they shattered. The forest needed thinning. The dead wood had to be cleared in case of fire; Ma Ferguson herself said so. Waste was by far the greater sin than theft, and charity was taken for granted. Poverty was a desirable state among the young, one striven for or, at the very least, simulated.

The Farm needed bodies and they found them: drifters and seekers, outcasts and mystics, people who knew how to slaughter a sheep and people who thought the world was about to end, clever people with big ideas who fought with Solly and left in a huff, people who believed in fresh air and clean food, people who had run out of money and ideas and were on their way somewhere else. Barefoot girls came with babies and sourdough starter. Boys with American accents and wonderful sneakers trudged in and refused to give their names. There were people who liked to build things and people who liked to cut things down. Some of them stole what little they had and were gone by morning and soon forgotten.

To all of them, Solly said, 'You are free here.' And nobody laughed.

In Solly's mind was a circle where the chickens turned weeds and scraps into manure and eggs, where the birds killed the bugs, where the sheep trimmed the grass and grew clean, perfect wool, where people were earnest and content, where children danced naked in the daisies and grew strong on love and good fresh food. He made quiet, sure speeches over coffee and put up a corkboard and posted lists of repairs to be made, skills to acquire: how to repoint mortar, shear a sheep, blanch celery, lay in irrigation; how to build a drystone wall and a split-rail fence, how to sharpen a saw; all this could be done with free labour and free labour was plentiful. Lists of what to barter for: salt, sugar, tobacco, milk, flour, spices, nails, coffee, seed, raisins, rope, creosote, bananas and oranges, how-to books, axe handles, sandpaper. But what to barter? eggs, flowers and vegetables, preserves, wool dyed with dandelion and blackberry and spun into lumpy yarn. Skills to be hired out: tutors and babysitters, handymen and gardeners.

Second-rate wood could be sold by the cord to those too rich or busy to do their own chopping. Better wood could be transformed, he dreamed, into something else. He kept the old tools to himself, and sanded them, oiled them, identified them, found their balance in his hand. He consulted the old-timers and scraped away at cedar and Douglas fir. He set others to mending fences and chopping wood.

He borrowed a *Sunset* book and built four plain, square, pale tables in the fashion of the time. But Solly's tables wobbled and people laughed and said he was no carpenter and waited for him to try something else. He scowled and snapped at Isobel and couldn't sleep nights. She would wake cold and alone in bed and would see the glow from the toolshed out the window. Strange shapes began to come out of the barn: bookcases made of the sinuous flaking limbs of arbutus that held books like offerings, tables that looked as if they could walk across the room, bentwood chairs from the local willows, naive and charming and pretty much expected to wobble. The local people laughed again and shook their heads, but not the tourists. The tourists bought.

It would take years for Solly to become technically

proficient, to master the perfect joint, the straight plumb, the mitred angle, but the eye was there from the beginning. Cabinetmaking came to him as if he had known it before. In twenty-five years, his work has progressed from the practical to the whimsical to the ironic to the surreal to the abstract, no longer sittable or sleepworthy, incapable of holding even a cup of coffee. But he trains his students to start as he did, with understanding of material, care of tools and respect for tradition. They build straight steady bookcases and plain parson's tables that never wobble. He understands that the kids need simple solid skills and that his vision is singular and non-negotiable.

They needed more people. People came. A girl who called herself Lifegiver came and planted by the moon and danced naked at midsummer and in spring watered the roses with her morning pee. Lifegiver worked all day in the hot garden and by candlelight read palms and skulls and tea leaves. She saluted the sun every morning and attributed magical properties to menstrual blood. She brandished an opinion on every subject and defended them all with the unshakeable faith of the strong of character or the hopelessly stupid. When Solly baited Lifegiver and laughed at her faddish pretensions, she stared him down with the opaque eyes of a fanatic. He tolerated her only because she knew how to grow vegetables. Never mind what incantations she mumbled over the peas, they grew strong and bore thickly even when summer came, long after the neighbours' peas were sere. Fancy cooks came to peer at the farm stand and pay a fortune for tiny wax potatoes and butter beans.

Lifegiver was thrilled with Isobel's pregnancy; she considered it the ultimate female experience. ('Unless you count death,' Solly muttered.) She fed Isobel like a bird on golden seeds and tender infant vegetables. She dangled a watch over her stomach and coveted the afterbirth.

'She's trouble,' Solly worried, sensing a coven in the making.

'She's harmless,' Isobel replied. Lifegiver stayed.

When people drifted away, they trolled for more at the Saturday market. Solly was strongly persuaded by physique. He looked for heavily built men and curvy women, claiming fleshy people were more tractable and worked harder too. Isobel was drawn to poets, people who sold painted rocks or bits of driftwood that looked a bit like Nixon or John Lennon. Solly looked for tree planters, fruit pickers, tradesmen with calloused hands and dirty fingernails, tans that ended above the eyes and biceps. Isobel looked for dreamers and doctors of philosophy. Booker used to say Solly was building a society and Isobel was building a zoo.

Solly rolled his eyes when she found Booker. 'I knew it,' he said. 'I could have picked him out a mile away.' He had been sizing up a buxom girl selling dandelion wine.

Booker simply stood there in the middle of the market with a plate of hash brownies in his hands. (The presence of hash was taken on trust; the high price was taken as proof. As it turned out, the brownies contained very little hash but who was to know? and, anyway, they were delicious. Later, she would catch him chopping Willow's brown crayon into the batter. 'It says non-toxic right on the box, Iz!' Sometimes, the crayons produced a spectacular high.)

Solly said he was the whitest person in the world. He had a thick rough freckled skin and his hair was frizzy and the colour of Orange Crush under a funny woollen hat of the kind that is knitted by grandmothers and deliberately lost by children on the first day of school.

The dandelion girl took off two days later with the egg money, but Booker stayed. He inspected the Farm in detail, unlike the others they brought home. 'Fantastic place to crash,' they would say. Booker didn't treat the Farm like a place to crash. He didn't think much of the weeds in the garden paths (Lifegiver was respectful of weeds) but he approved of the woodlot. He pronounced the chimneys sound and the well water sulphuric but potable – a question they had never considered; no one had got sick, had they? He found alarming signs of carpenter ants and pointed out that the bald eagles they had been admiring all summer were turkey vultures. (Isobel was devastated to learn that vultures and eagles were nearly indistinguishable from a distance and from then on never trusted those noble, floating shapes.)

Booker had a tendency to stare fixedly at people when they talked, as if he would hold them accountable for the most casual remark. He ate very slowly and thoroughly, chewing without expression, while the others got up and sat down, talked with their mouths full, choked and spluttered, had their backs pounded, explained at length why they weren't eating or argued just as persuasively why they were. As Isobel remembers Farm conversations, they are frenetic, rife with dissent; arguments last hours, days. People scream, laugh aloud, fall into each other's arms. She can see the scenes as in a film, but it's a foreign film; the actual words are unintelligible. What made the conversation memorable, Isobel thinks now, was not the subject matter, but the fervour of the discussion, the assumption that even trivia had weight and import, that no experience was unworthy of assessment.

Solly is dismissive; those vicious debates were about the exact lyrics of popular songs … *like about six months on 'American Pie'*, or whether a colour was blue or green. Once the Farm was abandoned, Solly chose to remember only the pointlessness of it.

There Isobel sat, a skinny girl gradually rounding out in pregnancy, listening rapt as they chattered about food, not knowing that food would become a major theme in her life, that the cycle of three square meals a day would turn and turn and turn, rolling over her again and again, not knowing then that she would produce more and more mouths to feed.

But in her youth, she felt privileged to soak the oatmeal overnight and the lentils all morning, to grind the spices and press the tofu. It felt important to do so.

There were those who brandished *Laurel's Kitchen* like a political tract and who regarded as poison flour that was not stone-ground and eggs that were anything but free-range. They preferred meditation to marijuana and mushroom tea to beer (though the effect was similar). They quarantined their food in a special corner of the fridge. What they ate tended to be very unstable and had to be acquired in minute amounts and gobbled up quickly before it fermented, separated or turned green; the fact that it was only briefly edible was considered proof of its wholesomeness. They favoured seeds and uncultured yogurt and honey from the very best bees and obscure whole grains with violent names like millet and rape. Solly deplored their diet as affectation and often mentioned livestock feed while in their company. Lifegiver would turn her big brown eyes on him and slowly chew as she described in detail the cancer that was nibbling at his colon.

As Isobel got fatter, the subject turned to childbirth.

'Women in China just squat in some ditch, wrap up the baby and go back to the rice paddy,' Elspeth said, Lifegiver said, even Isobel said. Childbirth, they insisted, was a natural process, elemental, as normal as a sneeze, a crap, a fuck. They were complacent, trustful of their women's bodies which, had never turned on them before.

As far as Solly was concerned, the women in China would take a nice, clean bed over a rice paddy any day. He wouldn't go along with any of it, not the herbs, not the incense, not the sound of the sea or the watery birth. He took Isobel to the doctor and fed her milk and spinach and vitamins they could barely afford. Sex became a stylized dance: Isobel, full of hormones and passion, rubbing her stomach against him as hard and resilient as a soccer ball, lying spread-eagled on the bed offering blue-veined breasts, Solly breathless and tentative, barely daring to stroke and penetrate this ripe new partner. He couldn't believe that the emergence of this huge growth would leave Isobel intact: bones would break, flesh would part. Tears and semen ran when they made love. He knew she was about to die.

She fell in love with herself pregnant. 'Are you resting?' he would ask, when he found her half asleep in the afternoon. 'No,' she would say. 'I'm busy at the moment. I'm very busy making something.' A smug little smile, her small face all eyes and cheekbones, her neck a line of poetry. She would break, he knew it.

She listened too much to Lifegiver. Lifegiver, who ate magic mushrooms and tiny bits of rhubarb leaf and couldn't remember where she came from, claimed to have delivered a hundred babies, 'all beautiful.'

'All healthy?' he snarled. 'All in one piece?'

Lifegiver nagged at Isobel about the gentle young doctor. 'Episiotomy,' she threatened. 'Anaesthetic. Forceps delivery. C-section just for the fun of it.'

When the contractions began, Solly had to kidnap her, pick her up and carry her past all the disapproving women so Willow could be born in the cool, clean, white hospital among people who knew their job. They let him hold her, just for a few minutes while they repaired the damage to Isobel. Then they told him to go away, so he did, and he cried and cried and cried.

It turned out that they were both right, the women and he: birth was perfectly normal and ordinary and, like many other ordinary events, it was tinged with magic and danger, an event so close to death he refused to watch it ever again.

Chapter Nine

Nancy was in on it. She told Isobel the day she met her that she had no use for hippies. No get-up-and-go, she said. Nancy was all go, a big square girl from a big, square island family; go from way back. While the proud and ambitious Fergusons had dwindled down to Ma in her trailer and Dean in Calgary, Nancy's great-grandfather had seen his dream of dynasty fulfilled. He came from Ireland, sailing around the Cape to Victoria. Just across the narrows, the government man said, pointing, there was good, cheap island land to be had for the clearing of it. Nancy's great-grandfather wasn't afraid of islands; a boundary of water could be a blessed protector as much as a means of exile.

He rowed himself across the narrows and gambled the last of his savings on three hundred acres of rolling cedar forest. He lived there alone for some years, fending off bears and cougars and nervously witnessing the territorial battles of the coastal Indian tribes from a mud-floored cabin in Murphy's Bay, clearing land, selling cedar shakes and moonshine until he'd saved up enough money to start a family. The land was nothing without children. Then, as was the custom, he dug out his musty woollen suit and went down to the wharf at the foot of the hill to meet the bride ship and pick out a wife. He looked for a strong, healthy woman; beauty and charm were luxuries beyond his means. He picked well: Mary bore sixteen children and raised ten, not a bad record. When the children were still very small, they worked the land and built the roads and helped to raise the school and then walked six miles through the woods to attend it. By that time the last of the bears had been shot, the fruit and nut trees were bearing and the family moonshine was reckoned the island's best. There was no dishonour in moonshining. As long as his whisky was safe and palatable, the moonshiner could be a rector of the church and his pretty daughters could dance the quadrille at Sir William Roberts' summer place in Driftwood, travelling sixteen miles by wagon to do so, frills and ribbons and satin slippers and all.

Nancy's grandfather had represented the island in the provincial legislature for three years until he was shot by a temperance advocate as he stepped off the barge *Isabella* one afternoon. Her father had noisily presented one of his many small islands to the Princess Elizabeth on the occasion of her marriage. She had turned around and given it to the province, but that didn't matter a whit on the island. A man who gave land to royalty was a man of stature.

It made Nancy an old-timer, an aristocrat of sorts. She was known and understood by her neighbours to the last microscopic thread of her DNA. She spoke plain like her father and his father. She had the Hubble jaw. In a place that attracted so many strangers, the familiar was revered.

She wore brand-name jeans and sweaters from mainland boutiques, and smirked at Isobel's granny boots and long cotton skirts. Nancy's children ate white bread and store-bought cookies and watched *The Friendly Giant* in colour and rode to school on a new yellow bus. Still, she was a farm girl and could birth a lamb if she had to. When one of the expensive new ewes began to bleed and Solly was looking it up in his farm management manual and Booker was checking *The Whole Earth Catalogue* and the others were standing around looking upset, Isobel grabbed Willow and sprinted across country to Nancy's new cedar-sided bungalow.

Nancy heard her out, then muttered and changed into old clothes and stomped over and turned the lamb around and pulled it out and gave them all a lecture on modern farming and scornfully refused the coffee, eggs, butter, flowers, and dried beans that were all they had to offer as payment. She made it clear that she didn't like them or what they stood for;

she suspected there was satire in the pastiche of farm life they were enacting. She mistrusted city people, was afraid of their glib conversation and pulsing, pointless energy. She resented their easy assumption that they could do, without training or experience, what her family had learned to do over a hundred years. City people had come before with their eyes full of daisies and their heads full of dreams. Then the tractor rolled or the woods burned or the chainsaw bucked and sliced into city sinew or just the sameness of the days wore away at their bright ideas and they slunk away. But neighbours, even hippies, were still neighbours and duty to neighbours had been ground into her from birth. You might not have spoken to him in years, but you would still put out your neighbour's barn fire and he yours.

She showed Isobel where the salmonberries grew and how to make the jam set. She brought over old receiving blankets and bunting bags for Willow, and later, winter coats and gum boots. She wouldn't come into the house – too disorganized, she claimed – and on those days when Isobel agreed with her, she'd stick Willow in Nancy's old baby carriage and trudge up the road to sit in Nancy's centrally heated house and listen to the throb of electric appliances and consider the advantages of hot water heaters and TV sets.

She tried to avoid Nancy's husband, Gene, a leering beanpole who didn't mind hippies in the least. He liked to drop by without warning in the hope of catching them, they assumed, orgiastic or merely whimsically naked. He'd heard, old Gene, about communes, and his nasty little eyes fumbled over braless breasts under old T-shirts and, if you weren't quick, his hands followed: bralessness was permission. At home he was utterly benign, wiping his boots on the mat without fail and supporting Nancy in a strictly adhered-to scheme for the acquisition of household furnishings, the latest colour, the most exciting gadgetry much debated and pleasurably analysed. The nubby oatmeal couch from Sears replaced Gene's mother's old chesterfield, which Solly was permitted to haul away so he could strip it to its frame and study its bone structure. The wall-to-wall and curtains to match; the lamps and pillows in carefully considered contrast, the spare and ruthlessly tidy house attested to their management and good taste. When Nancy couldn't sleep, she got up and rearranged the furniture.

The farm got the old furniture: two kitchen chairs, an iron floor lamp, some art-nouveau prints that were entirely too fanciful for the time, an inlaid mahogany table with a wobbly leg. Isobel was ashamed and protested that Solly could repair the table, but Nancy wouldn't have it back. It refused to match; it was too fussy and spindle-legged, the mahogany was too dark: the squat beige lamp from the Bay demanded stripped pine. So the pretty little table went to the Farm with its plank-and-brick bookcases, its armchairs that coughed up stuffing and dust, its oak bedsteads and dressers that had been left in the abandoned house only because they were too heavy to haul away.

Nancy could predict hard winters and the gender of unborn babies. She could calm horses and find groundwater. She could cure warts and brew an abortifacient. She could curse you if she felt inclined.

She said the farm was cursed.

'What happened?' Isobel asked.

'Nothing yet. You keep a close eye on that baby though. There's a child in it somewhere.'

So when Isobel looked out the window and saw the cougar, just its hindquarters and the long rope of tail, it was the curse she thought of first. A half hour earlier she had put Willow down in a basket on the front porch and − yes, she was still there, wrapped up like a loaf of bread, asleep. She looked again at the animal. It might have been a yellow Lab but for the tail and the careful feline tread. As she watched, it slipped into the fringe of broom at the forest's edge a field away.

Solly's buddies at the general store liked to tell cougar stories. They were old-timers mostly, too old to do much but growl out their acquired wisdom. They preferred to talk of the past when they were young and vital, rather than the present in which they were at the mercy of women, wives and daughters. They were fond of cougar stories; the island was an unusually benign environment and these pioneers liked to play up the occasional threat, which was exactly what the cougar was. There were no colonies left on Lost Answers, but every few years a young male would swim across the strait in search of new territory and would have to be hunted down and killed.

A cougar will take down an eight-year-old. A snack. They prefer their dinner to wriggle on the way down, the old-timers said. *A cougar will kill a man if he has to. You never meet the eyes of a cougar, but you never turn and run either: watch a tabby with a mouse if you don't believe it. You stand your ground and hold your arms over your head. You want to look as big as you can when you meet a cougar.*

Isobel stood beside the baby carriage and gazed at the woods a field away, woods that went on for a mile and a half until the sea put a stop to it, woods that until today had been as harmlessly agreeable as a theme park. She reviewed the conventional wisdom.

There are no cougars here.

If there was a cougar, everyone would know about it. Deer would have been found slashed apart. Sheep and dogs and domestic cats would have gone missing. What she saw was a yellow Lab. What she saw was someone's pony; even now there were children looking for it. There are no cougars here.

She snatched Willow awake from a deep sleep, and ran into the house with the screaming baby and slammed the door tight. There was no lock. Why was there no lock? The new girl from Oregon wandered downstairs, puffy with sleep, and squealed as Isobel wrenched her arm.

'Go and find Solly and tell him I just saw a cougar go into the woods.'

The girl's eyes lit up. 'Wow!' she cried. She ran outside to look. 'Where?' She'd get her camera in a minute.

'GET SOLLY!' Isobel screamed above the baby's racket.

He came eventually, smiling his amused disbelief. They were forced to shout at each other to be heard over Willow; all three red-faced and desperate as if they were engaged in a vicious domestic argument, until Booker took Willow away upstairs and stood with her by a window and pointed out the raindrops on the glass, the breeze in the trees.

Because he'd been shouting, Solly's heart pounded, and he felt the need to address Isobel's panic and not the unlikely possibility of the cat. He held her by the shoulders. He spoke slowly and calmly. He told her to sit down.

She shoved him away and stepped back to minimize his advantage in size. She fixed him with her eye.

'Shut up and get the man,' she said. 'Right now.'

The cougar man was red-faced and work-knotted. He held a shotgun over his left elbow, barrels broken open, and a pair of large, solemn dogs waited for orders at his feet. He had a gleam in his eye that Isobel understood. This calm solid island man would do her killing for her.

'That beast's ten miles gone by now, if he's here. If he's here, the dogs'll find him.'

Solly caught the gleam and picked it up and followed. Two men, two dogs, calm and grim, not quite believing but ready for anything. She watched as they trudged off: the doubt in their bowed heads, the grim set of the shoulders. She was satisfied.

Booker brought Willow back downstairs for a feed. Around her, the others debated the rights of animals and the rights of man. Most, who hadn't seen the cougar, who didn't have a potential snack in the form of a child, who would be gone in a month anyway, were immovably on the side of the animal. Man and beast should co-exist, they declared. There was the SPCA. There were humane traps. What about the balance of nature? Man had raped and pillaged enough. (Man, as a concept, was much maligned at the farm.) They elected to track Solly and the cougar man so that they could intervene between cougar and gun, or if need be, cougar and dog. (They knew nothing about hunting and were unsure of the details.) They felt the cougar, even as it died, should be made to feel their empathy. Isobel sat and cupped Willow's furry head and felt the tingle as the milk let down and spurted out of her and waited for the sound of the shot.

The others never left; the issue was too fraught with opinion for that; it was the debate rather than the action that mattered. In the end, the cougar was treed and killed too far away for them to hear the sound of its death. Someone from the weekly paper came out and took a picture and there next week were the man and Solly, grinning, with seven feet of cat between them. The man was thrifty with the kill, Solly reported, steeped now in the lore. He would sell the pelt and feed the meat to the dogs. The grandchildren could have the teeth for show-and-tell. The bones would be scattered around the vegetable garden to frighten the deer.

And the woods were safe again. Nancy was wrong.

Chapter Ten

Pat has brought vodka.

'Has she called yet?'

'No. Nothing. But then that's Maggie. A real pain in the ass.' Isobel sighs gustily. She's not used to drinking and will begin to feel sick in a minute. 'How did this happen? I was only trying to do the right thing.'

'Yeah, well, that's written on a lot of headstones.'

'Why can't they find her? What's so hard about finding her? Am I getting too loud? Shut the door, I'll scare the kids.'

She begins to pace, moving too fast, speaking too fast. 'I'll just have to go down to the States myself, that's all. I'll have to do the fucking job for them.'

'Are you sure they'll let you out of the country?' Pat asks gently.

Isobel seems not to hear this. 'What if she's dead? What if she's killed herself?' Tears flow. 'Don't let me drink any more.'

'It was supposed to be an anaesthetic.'

Pat has heard from the Neighbourhood. The Neighbourhood feels betrayed. It has put its trust in Solly and Isobel; put up with, even envied them, their quirks, and it is now clear that it has been duped. It turns out that Solly and Isobel are just as rotten as everyone else. There's talk now at dinner parties of sweatshops. People are quick to point out a long-held but unspoken suspicion.

The hydro bill is due.

Larry King has called.

Solly's timber merchant has left four messages.

The turnout at the L.A. retrospective was disappointing but Bill has high hopes for Chicago and New York where, he says, they're not overburdened with guilt.

Jerry Springer has called.

Magnolia's on the cover of *Rolling Stone.*

Solly's never home. He's looking for warehouse space in Richmond. He wants to open a factory using the students to turn out reproductions of his work. Somewhere he's picked up a jargon that includes profit margins and GST refunds. He's become concerned about the state of his clothes and he keeps saying *Let's be sensible.* He's given up smoking. He seems smaller somehow.

Pat's daughter, Megan, is the only paying student Solly has left and now even Megan's father is grumbling about the fees. Let him grumble, Pat says spitefully. The money's half hers. She'll pay the tuition herself if she has to. But only if she has to.

When Megan heard of the Project, she wanted it with the same ferocious lust she'd exhibited over the years for a red velvet party dress, a Victorian dollhouse, a pony, a Jeep. It was this ruthless egoism that persuaded Pat that there was hope for Megan yet. Now again here was something Megan wanted and Pat suspected that the something was a man.

There was an opening at an edgy gallery on lower Granville Street. A chair had just been listed in the Pace Gallery catalogue and this was the place to be, this man was a man to meet. There he was: a burly figure in a mouldy old sweater with a bottle of Blue in his hand. He turned to look at Pat as she spoke, then he stared, and she realized he needed her like a meal or a breath. She was thirty-eight and had married out of high school. She'd grown accustomed to indifference from men. No one had ever needed her as much as food and air.

They found a taxi and a room. He pored over her; he absorbed her; he divined her smallest inclination. Briefly, she was the most important woman in the world and she glowed like a candle until he told her, two weeks later, that he'd found another woman he needed more.

Enraged with grief and dressed to kill, she stormed the house the next day. *I never seduce my students. The students are different. That's work.* She would see about that. The man was a monster.

She jammed her thumb into the doorbell button and kept it there. And summoned Isobel, barefoot in a stained skirt and washed-out, stretched-out T-shirt. Small and beautiful children appeared around her legs where they clung open-mouthed, like sea anemones.

'I want to see Solly,' Pat announced. 'I'm Megan's mother.'

'Yes,' Isobel said, looking her up and down. 'My name is Isobel. You should come in.' But there wasn't really enough hall to come in to, and Isobel and the children had to step sideways into a bizarre painted room before leading her into a kitchen that smelled of cigarettes and bread.

'Sorry,' Isobel said, pushing random clutter aside on the kitchen table. 'Sorry. We haven't cleaned up yet. It's pretty awful.'

It was pretty awful. There was a humid sneaker on the table. There was also a jar of jam, two spoons, four felt-tip markers and two felt-tip marker tops, an eggcupful of wilted pansies, and a stringed instrument, possibly a cello.

'Sorry, sorry,' Isobel kept saying, scooping stuff up and piling it high on an already teetering heap in a laundry basket.

She'd expected a shrew, or a shapeless heap, or a jolly, asexual camp counsellor, not this ragged sylph.

'Solly says Megan's doing very well. He says she's got a good eye and she isn't afraid of hard work.'

'I want to talk to him.'

Isobel slid a cup of coffee in front of Pat and sat down. 'Sure you do, but it won't make any difference. And there's Megan. As I said, Megan's doing really well. She's involved out there. She's interested. Screaming at Solly won't do anything. It might hurt. If it's Megan you're worried about. It *is* Megan, right?'

Pat tried the coffee. She'd drunk coffee black for years and this was strong and sweet with sugar and cream and it tasted like a revelation. Pat was afraid of Megan. There'd been a frightening bout of anorexia some years back. There was a picture she couldn't quite blank out of a wooden spoon jammed between Megan's clenched teeth and the fear and rage that powered the arm that held it.

'Of course it's about Megan. I have a right to know what she's doing here.'

Isobel lit a cigarette and resented Pat's cream wool suit. Pat wasn't the first bitter discard she'd had to cope with.

She could understand the attraction. Pat was polished. Polished and burnished and ever so carefully rubbed. When men spoke of women aging like wine, was this, a woman whose face betrayed no past at all, what they meant? Where were you in '72? she wanted to ask. Here was a person who had chosen to erase the map on her face.

'You'll just embarrass her if you go out there. You know you will. She's doing fine. She's getting along with the other kids. She's learning skills. She's good with numbers, did you know that?'

'Of course I know that. I'm her mother.'

At the same moment, they dropped their eyes to the table. Pat wished she had a drink. Isobel was thankful she didn't.

'I can't guarantee that chair's clean,' she said finally. 'That's a gorgeous suit.' She resisted the impulse to scream shut up at Mick and a school friend who were amusing themselves upstairs, apparently by dropping a bowling ball from a great height.

'It can be cleaned,' Pat replied, not even looking. And she didn't flinch when Toby wandered in and leaned against her thigh, leaving behind a water stain and the smell of pee.

'I think I need a cigarette.'

Isobel handed her the pack.

Pat lit a cigarette with amateurish ceremony. She could just see the garage though the window in the kitchen door. Solly was in the garage. But by now there was a spot of coffee and a lot of cigarette ash on her new suit. 'So clean,' he had murmured, running his hand up a well-muscled, waxed and mud-bathed thigh. 'So manicured, so pedicured, so well-tended. Like a bonsai.' She was still well-tended. The suit could be cleaned. The new woman was what? unwashed? unbrushed? untended? like a weed?

'So this is how it works? You clean up after him?'

'Every single fucking time.'

This time, they looked up.

At some point, the kitchen had been painted black and the cabinet doors covered with still lifes of fruits and vegetables, a few nudes. She thought of her own tidy house, carefully decorated by a friend of a friend, of Peter's study with its Persian rug and maroon walls, its gleaming shelves of leatherbound books bought in bulk, its pictures of large sailboats lurching around in terrible weather.

'I like this kitchen,' she allowed.

'Solly's aunt started it, and then she gave the kids a cabinet each. Ash did the top ones,' Isobel said. Isobel thought the top ones were pretty good.

'I hardly go into mine,' Pat confessed, 'except when we're having a small dinner party. I like cooking for those. The large ones are catered, of course, and we eat out a lot. The cook takes care of the everyday.'

'Does she?' Isobel asked. She got up and began to chop vegetables in a showy manner although she didn't have to for another half hour.

'Do you have any questions about the Project? It's not just that we need the tuition, although we do. But Megan's doing fine, really.'

'I've heard the philosophy.'

Of course she had. Isobel's face closed and she began to destroy a bunch of celery.

'I mean, your husband did mention that some of the students are socially disadvantaged.'

'Some of the kids are addicts and they either quit while

they're here or we get them into treatment, which isn't always easy. Some were prostitutes. Girls and boys. We've had our share of AIDS cases.'

'AIDS! What about your own kids?'

Isobel put the cleaver down very carefully. 'The AIDS kids are not even remotely threatening to little kids, unless they're already so sick they're irrational and then we don't take them. It's the possible sexual partners we have to worry about, that and sharing needles. Every kid – and I mean every kid, Granville Street or Kerrisdale – is tested every month and lectured constantly and we practically upholster the place with condoms. The thing is, you can't stop sex. Sex happens, right? But it shouldn't kill you. We think Megan's handling the situation well, but if it concerns you, you should take her out. I would.'

'Right,' Pat said, standing up and brushing ash off her skirt, 'I might do that.'

'Think about it.'

But Pat didn't take Megan out. A week later she appeared again, in jeans this time (although they were ironed jeans, possibly dry-cleaned, Isobel noted, subtracting marks).

'Actually, I brought over some clothes we don't wear anymore. I thought some of the kids might ...'

'You're kidding me,' Isobel purred. 'Where are they?'

'I left them in the car. I wasn't sure ...'

'Oh, you don't have to spare our feelings,' Isobel said, walking to the top of the basement stairs. 'We basically don't have any.' Without pausing, she raised her voice to a bellow. 'Who's home?'

A little voice squeaked.

'No, not you. I need someone big. Find me someone a lot bigger ... Well, tell him it's your Lego, too.'

She turned back to Pat. 'Is the car locked? One of the kids will get the stuff. Did you put in any men's clothes? It's the boys that need them. The girls will go without food to have clothes, but the boys don't care. As a matter of fact, Solly wouldn't turn down a comfortable shirt.'

'I didn't think of men,' Pat replied weakly, cowed in the face of such greed. 'I can see what Peter doesn't need.' She considered Peter's closet. All those shoes. All those shoe-trees. Peter disapproved of non-deductible charity. If she took shoes, she'd have to take shoe-trees too.

'You've got guts, I'll give you that,' Isobel conceded. 'None of the parents ever come here twice.'

'I do have guts,' Pat said. 'I used to like Solly. Now I like you.'

'Yup, same old story. You wouldn't believe how many girl-friends I have.'

Pat let out a high shriek that woke Toby up from his nap.

And now Pat puts Isobel to bed and caps the vodka bottle and orders six large pizzas from the Brick Oven and puts out plates and napkins and lets Toby and Monty watch something not on Channel 9 and allows Winnie to tell her about the science fair and grabs Solly's hand as he passes and says something flippant and tries to remember what she saw in him. Whatever it was is gone.

Chapter Eleven

She knows by their speculative glances that the flight attendants have recognized her, if not exactly as Frances Lamb, then at least as someone of consequence. This is becoming increasingly common: people know her but can't place her; the face is remembered, the feat forgotten. She could be a character actress. Or *actor*, she corrects herself. (She's secretly uneasy with this new language, fearing that the upholstery of the sharp edge will only serve to disguise it and make it more dangerous.)

Nevertheless, she aims a smile at the nearest flight attendant. *I'm the reason you're not a stew any more.*

She pulls out her speech. She's opening this conference. This is another thing that's happening more and more; she's writing the foreword rather than the thesis. Still, a speech is a speech and Frances is an old pro: important points are highlighted in yellow, pauses are marked in blue. No one can fault it. She gives it a fond little pat.

She looks out the window at the empty landscape. Frances despises Vancouver, such a silly place with its gaudy setting and its bafflingly smug people. Not a serious place at all. No bustle, no edge and as cold as death. Her good, sensible clothes are suddenly inappropriate in Vancouver, her coat too thick, her dress too thin. At the conference, the women will be calm, fat and philosophical. If she didn't have to deal with Magnolia and Isobel, she wouldn't even be on the plane.

She's becoming tired of her children and their expectations. If she's old – and she is – then her kids are middle-aged. It's past time they had the ideals knocked off them. She'd had the war, though, both an excuse to be reckless and a reason to grow up.

Even her children don't know she's been married twice. She

discarded that episode when she met Duncan and emigrated to Canada. The first one's name was Frank Martin, Frank and Frances; that was the joke – their mothers said it was meant. He was just a boy of twenty, but then she was a girl of eighteen; strange how she remembers herself as so grown up, much like she is now in fact, and yet he, long-lashed, shy, gangly, seems so ridiculously young in recollection. They had fallen in love, if a few shared discoveries, a few chaste kisses, a few coincidences of interest and experience, can be defined as love. At least they had called it that.

They had married, he a soldier, she a canteen worker; they had married quickly, assured of eternal love but insuring against the war. And Frank was killed six months later, before she even felt like a proper married lady, before she had moved out of her parents' little house, or had to scrounge up furniture or learn to cook, before she could choose the kind of crockery she would like and place it before him of an evening with whatever she could make of the ration. They hadn't even played house, she and Frank, which was why she so often forgot him and perhaps why she kept him a secret from Duncan and the children. Even when she became the Famous Frances, it was a giggle to keep that one little passage from all the people who thought they read her like a book.

Maybe it was the war. To survive a war is to know how absurdly easy it is to die. You can die over dinner, you can die on the toilet. All the old rules are broken and suddenly everyone is someone else. Princesses fix cars and typists take to the land. Pink little schoolboys become heroes or corpses. It isn't like real life at all. Real life anticipates a future and behaves with decorum. War life is careless and not a thing you discuss with the children.

The mothers were devastated, of course. This was what all mothers feared, and why not? Imagine the horror of it, a child blown to bits, burned beyond recognition, often simply sucked into foreign soil. Frank's mother coped brightly; thrust herself into charitable works, bustled about growing thinner and thinner. Her own mother merely held her and wept. Frances wasn't sure what to feel. Frank had died. They had known this might happen. In their nine days as man and wife, a week and two days' leave, they had talked about it, but not seriously. It wasn't a serious time. They had drunk beer and toasted the widow Martin.

It was easy, once he was gone, to imagine that he had never been. Or it would have been easy, but for the mothers, who smiled like conspirators and remarked on her rosiness, her general laxity, attributing loss and confusion to pregnancy. It took her some weeks to catch on to this, but once she did, she played up: took to feeling faint in the morning and drowsy in the afternoon, began to crave funny foods at funny times, just to give the mothers something to be happy about, especially Mrs Martin; Frances's heart lurched over Mrs Martin, who had loved Frank so much more than she did. Some kind of promise, even a false one, seemed appropriate.

Frances realizes she's doing this more often these days, taking out her old memories and airing them like yellowed linen. Frank has been put away for fifty years, and here he is as fresh and young as ever. Fresher than yesterday.

Just last week, in the middle of dressing down the minister, she forgot his name. And he, a man her son's age but seeming older with that portly avuncularity even teenage politicians like to cultivate, had the gall to be tactful about it. She had to storm out of his office, shaking with fear. Going forward is all she knows.

She reads through the speech again. She can still rouse the rabble all right. That's still with her.

All her life, Frances has drawn her sense of purpose and duty from beliefs as still and pure as good well water. Even the most complex issue, a moral labyrinth to most, is to Frances a stretch of prairie road. This is her strength: that there is right and there is wrong and she is right. Although twenty years of lobbying have taught her to be cunning – she can wring a useful contact dry and attract a scrum in her sleep – she never fails to speak her mind, even when it would be wiser to hold her tongue. She knows it's led to a gentle nudging aside as women behind her, her younger colleagues, slip past her wielding reasoned compromise while she, the anachronism, sticks to strident confrontation. Now she's brought out ceremonially, like an old veteran on Remembrance Day, scarred and bemedalled, symbol of a war won long ago, while the modern army quietly pushes buttons and dances like a diplomat.

So Frances, the old trouper, soars over the wide wintry land and flexes her feet in her sensible shoes and goes over her speech once more. It's nearly time to come down.

Picture this: a conference, Women of the Nineties – even the title is a little quaint. A three-day conference, with the opening address given by Frances, the keynote speaker a conspicuously well-preserved American politician wearing silk and fuck-me shoes. Frances, true to form, is quotable and colourful. If a reporter mentions Magnolia she makes him feel like a piece of shit.

Picture this: she arrives exhausted after taking the bus from her hotel – it's part of Frances's code to use public transit whenever possible. Isobel opens the door to Frances Lamb, public harridan, a person much larger than the woman herself. By the time the door closes, she's imploded, she's a little thing, slightly stout, no more than that, a surprisingly shrivelled nut inside a handsome shell.

She slumps at the kitchen table for an hour or two, while Isobel fearfully feeds her tea and toast, and how she goes on about that American woman's clothes. How could she march? How could she sit in? Frances will still go miles to sit in. In a loud, hurt voice she is grossly unfair to the woman whose most grievous fault is likely her nationality. (Frances is a career anti-American.)

She ignores the children who barge in demanding food and attention. Frances, after all, raised four children back in the days when husbands didn't help even if they hadn't disappeared. Her years of child-rearing she now recalls as a series of tiresome but simple chores and small events, forgetting, as mothers tend to, the wrenching immediacy of the job.

Isobel is jittery after a morning spent preparing earthquake comfort bags for Toby, Suzannah and Mick. Next year, she'll have to do it all over again. She's spent the morning in a crumpled world where hundreds are dead and thousands are lost under rubble, a world without heat, water, power, medical aid, a world where school buildings have turned to powder. Mothers are told to prepare for the predicted massive earthquake by packing candies and small cuddly toys and little notes into freezer bags which will be handed out by the teacher should the whole city collapse. Mothers write the notes again and again, in careful block letters for the little ones, until at last they manage to get one free of tear stains. *I love you. I'll come for you no matter what. I'll be there as soon as I can.*

They hear there's a secret list of the order in which the schools will fall down. (The mothers say it in whispers so the kids won't hear.) When they go and shriek, as some do, at school board meetings, they're told to behave themselves, that to shore up the heavy precarious buildings is too expensive to contemplate against an event that may not even happen. They're chided for their selfishness. There are children without lunches, winter coats, safe places to sleep. And what can they say to that? So the mothers pretend that by stocking the treacherous buildings with water and dust masks and comfort bags, their children will be safe, just as small Isobel was once taught that she would be safe from a nuclear bomb if she put enough practice into hiding under her desk.

Isobel tells Frances all about the comfort bags, expecting her to be outraged, to fire off faxes like bullets. But Frances can't seem to take in the comfort bags, doesn't notice Isobel's brimming eyes, forgets about Magnolia, develops chills and has to be put to bed. Frightened, Isobel dispatches the children in shifts to bring her chirpy news of the outside and sickroom food on trays. She gets a student to buy the *Globe and Mail* (without which Frances claims to be unable to start her day), and sits with her mother when she can, but she's busy, busy with all those small immediate events while her mother, suddenly not busy, stays in bed, catching up on twenty years of meetings, jet lag and bad food. Isobel has to force herself to find time for her mother who is suddenly not her mother. She feels the grasp of Frances's soft old hand every time she must leave, begging her to stay a little while, stay and talk, talk about anything, so she does, perched on the bed, and chatters as if nothing is wrong and needs her mother back, right now, not this feeble old woman who's forgotten her job.

And Frances does come back. There's a return ticket in her purse and, on the morning of her departure, she's herself again, up and dressed for the airport in stout winter boots and a green knit dress, her hair combed even at the back, carrying the impossibly warm coat in which she will arrive in Ottawa. Isobel won't have to call a family conference. Her mother is not her child any longer, but that relationship is ahead of her now like a landmark on a revised map.

Nervously, not trusting in Frances's recovery, Isobel insists on seeing her off at the airport although she knows that her mother prefers to slip cleanly into the traveller's tetherless mode. Frances carries a backpack and her small suitcase; her tickets are just where they should be; so are her thriller and Lifesavers.

Seeing someone off means little these days – no gangplanks, no handkerchiefs waved by shrinking figures, just brisk good-byes at the metal detector, a sense of holding up the line, a denial of sentiment in a crush of strangers.

They are quiet, patient, resigned, this crowd. The procedure is familiar to them. The only possible excitement is too frightening to think about. The very tedium of the exercise is reassuring.

Isobel and Frances shuffle toward the metal detector, breaking the silence with trite remarks, the time for intimacy past. The little boys keep slipping off between legs like fish among reeds and Isobel has trouble keeping them in sight.

Suddenly there's noise. Behind them approach the overly loud voices of young men with more energy than it's possible to expend in an airport. They can hear them coming – not quite boisterous, but certainly unreserved. People in line turn their heads to look back down the hall to the bend where the noise is coming from. A school group of skiers, Isobel guesses, watching for them too. A hockey team.

And then they burst around the corner in a tight, fast group, still laughing amongst themselves, still insulting each other, moving fast on strong sure legs, soldiers. There they are in their nothing-coloured uniforms and pale blue berets: Canadian soldiers embarking on a peace mission. And immediately all the eyes slide away and all the heads turn back and the soldiers are quiet and chastened, well-behaved boys. There has been trouble with one of the missions, bad trouble. This does not accord with the national desire to please.

The soldiers' eyes fall as they join the line-up.

Isobel locates Monty and Toby again, then turns back and sees Frances staring at the soldiers. Now, Frances puts her pack down emphatically, a piece of stage business if Isobel ever saw one. The people behind her hesitate and shuffle around her. Isobel senses an impending statement. She tightens the muscles of her neck.

The Famous Frances opens her mouth. Isobel nearly claps her hand over it. Even worse than a stained international reputation is embarrassment in any form. Please, she begs silently. Don't humiliate these boys. Don't humiliate me.

Frances speaks in her public voice, consonants snapping like new elastic. 'These young men ...' she begins. She has preserved and maintained her English accent. People listen to an English accent. The soldiers look up like little boys expecting punishment. 'These men,' she corrects herself firmly, 'are Canadian peacekeepers.'

Now the whole crowd has stopped, eyes down, ready to flinch.

'They are soldiers whose duty is to stop war, to prevent killing and cruelty. I think,' and here she looks around at her fellow travellers, 'that we should be proud of every one of them.' And slowly, loudly, she begins to clap. The soldiers redden and examine their boots. Monty joins in, clapping fast and jumping up and down. Passengers coming to join the line stop at the corner, not sure whether to join the crowd, wary of an incident.

'Yes,' someone says finally. 'Hear, hear,' says an older man. And one by one, the people in the line raise their heads and begin to applaud as the soldiers shuffle and turn even redder, their acne livid, and eventually begin to grin.

At precisely the moment when the sentiment begins to lose its freshness, Frances announces, 'They have important work to do. We mustn't delay them any longer. Let's move along.' And she picks up her backpack and turns toward the metal detector. 'That's Frances Lamb,' someone says. 'Remember her?'

Isobel kisses her goodbye. 'You're insane,' she whispers. Frances puts her backpack on the conveyor belt and leans over to wipe Isobel's face with a Kleenex found at the speed of light. 'Why is it,' she murmurs, 'that soldiers always have such terrible skin?' And she strides through the little tunnel, picks up her pack, blows a kiss to the kids, turns her back and walks away.

Isobel retrieves the boys and sidles through the line. Now the soldiers are having their hands shaken and their backs slapped. They are calling people *ma'am* and *sir* and they look like the embarrassment may kill them before they even reach the war zone. They want this over with, now. But they will remember it, all the same. It may be the only parade they will ever get.

So Frances is still Frances and Isobel is still busy with groceries and kids to pick up and Magnolia perhaps gone forever and a soccer game after school and by the time she gets home she has convinced herself that her mother's collapse was due to fatigue and nothing more.

It doesn't last. She has to strip the sheets so Ash and Pierre can move back in. She discovers the little cache between the sheets at the foot of the bed – crusts of toast, half a cookie, three linty Lifesavers, tucked away, hidden there as if they're worth taking, as if someone in the house might want them, as if Frances feared more food might never come in those days of collapse between the Hotel Vancouver and the airport.

It takes all afternoon to master the panic, doling out the after-school crackers and cheese, standing in a drizzle beside the muddy soccer field watching as Mick's team wins yet again, telling herself that her mother is fine, she was tired, that's all, she's as fine as she's ever been. So what if she forgot to brush her hair at the back so it stayed flattened by sleep until Isobel fluffed it for her? Of course she hadn't forgotten the existence of the back of her head. It's only a comfort bag, not an earthquake.

'Your face is wet,' Monty complains.

'So's yours. Pull your hood up,' she says.

Chapter Twelve

'Please just tell us exactly what happened, Ms Lamb. There's no hurry. In your own words.'

She laughs. 'That's just what the reporters say. You sound exactly like them.'

He looks like a nice man. His nails are bitten; she takes comfort in that. 'Just tell us what happened,' he persists.

So she does.

'What made you do it?' He sounds genuinely curious.

'I had to. She was mine. I loved her. I saved her. No one else loved her enough to do it. Everyone else was going to take the easy way out and do what they called the right thing. They didn't love her, so the right thing was easy.'

'So you don't deny you kidnapped her?'

'Well, of course not. It's obvious I did, isn't it? It must be on record. I want to know what you're doing about finding Magnolia. It should be easy. She's famous. My daughter's famous. Don't you realize that?'

'All I can tell you is that if the FBI can't find her, nobody can.'

'The FBI?' She's so startled, she laughs.

'Well, yes. She disappeared in the States. And it looks as if by rights she's an American citizen. So it's the FBI. We're in close contact but it's pretty much out of our hands.'

'Why can't they find her? What's wrong with them?'

'Do you have a lawyer, Ms Lamb?'

Solly clears his throat. 'We're seeing one this afternoon.'

'Good.' Isobel can sense that there are lots of masculine things not being said here. She can almost read the words that float across the table, words like take and charge, proper and procedure, protect and rights.

You're permitted to smoke in the police interview room.

You're encouraged to do so. The ashtray is slid your way. Matches and cigarettes are available. 'Do a lot of criminals smoke?' she asks. The men allow that to pass.

He begins again, 'Now, Ms Lamb, the house in which you reside belongs to you?'

'Yes.'

'Not to your common-law husband, Ingersoll Whitechapel?'

'No.'

'And yet it was left to you by his aunt, am I right?'

'Yes. She left it to me alone. You can check the will.'

'Why would she leave it to you and not to her own nephew who was also living there?'

'I have no idea. I guess I always assumed it was a woman thing. She was a single woman. She'd had to look after herself all her life. Maybe she thought I should have some property. I didn't even know until the will was read. And it didn't bother Solly, if that's what you're thinking.' She looks at him. 'Did it?'

'Of course not. I don't see where we're going here. This isn't anything to do with Maggie.'

'I understand that Winifred Whitechapel died in the house while under your care.'

'She had cancer.' Solly says with some belligerence.

'Yes. I've seen the death certificate. Smoke?'

She's got a lawyer. Her own lawyer, think of it. It seems pretentious even to need one. She and Solly wait in the reception room under the supervision of his nice crisp secretary. There's no smoking here. This is where criminals come, she tells herself, imagining criminals leafing through the *Financial Post* or *Harper's* under the scrupulously massed architectural prints. The presence of criminals seems much less likely here than in the grimy police station. Solly paces back and forth and occasionally says something like what if or maybe we could.

She says wait and see. She has faith in the famous lawyer Pat has called in.

Once they're allowed to see him, she's surprised by how small he is. He's only as tall as Isobel and not much heavier. His posture, however, is excellent. The nuns would approve.

He proceeds to grill her cruelly. He's much meaner than the cops.

'Look, I did what I thought was right, doesn't that count? If we hadn't taken her, she'd have been fostered out. Maybe for years.'

'You disapprove of foster homes, then?'

'Of course not! No, wait a minute, I take that back. Yes, I do. And so do you, if you're honest. And so does everybody else. Yes, they're wonderful people for the most part and what would society do without them, but would you want your kids in one?'

'But Magnolia wasn't your kid, was she?'

'She *was* my kid. I saved her. Look, I've already explained this to the police. I was the one who loved her. Without me, they'd have done the right thing. The right thing isn't always right, you know. What I did was illegal, I know that, but it wasn't wrong. I was the only one who loved her enough to break the law. Why doesn't anyone *get* that?'

Pat says this guy can pick and choose his cases and he likes this one, he's attracted to splashy cases. Pat says he's wily and ruthless and as slick as Vaseline.

'Isobel, clearly you don't understand the law. People don't. The law has nothing to do with right or wrong. The law's about regulation, not philosophy. The province doesn't care why you did it. They just have to prove you broke the law. What you did was illegal.'

'But not wrong,' she insists.

He exchanges a look with Solly and rubs his forehead.

Solly says, 'What's the big deal? It was years ago. What about the statute of limitations?'

'Not for kidnapping. Kidnapping's big time. Those sanctimonious bastards aren't going to let this one go.'

He turns back to Isobel and tries again. 'Okay, let's look at it another way. You kidnapped Magnolia because you believed it was the right thing to do even though you knew full well that it was against the law. Does that statement accurately reflect your state of mind at the time?'

'Yes,' she answers carefully, expecting a trap, a magical rabbit of a trick.

'Therefore, we must assume that you were prepared to pay for your actions. And now the law expects you to pay.'

She takes her time to think about it. This is a view she has never seen before, like an everyday object photographed at extreme magnification.

'I knew that if I was caught I might be sent to jail. I understood it was a crime. But I tried really hard not to be caught. I took Solly's name. The kids took his name. It actually wasn't that hard. People were always fooling around with names in the seventies. We just all became Whitechapels when we got to Vancouver. Nobody blinked an eye.'

'But the point is that you were prepared to go to jail in order to, as you put it, save Magnolia,' he insists.

'No. That's not right. I wasn't prepared to go to jail. I had three little kids. And I didn't save Magnolia just to have her taken away again. I didn't save her just to lose the others. I saved her because I was the only one there who loved her enough to save her. I wanted to save Magnolia. I wanted to keep my kids. Are you getting me here?'

'So you wanted to break the law and at the same time avoid being punished for it.'

'Don't good intentions count?'

'Not much.'

'That's shitty.'

'Isobel, you don't have a defence here. That's shitty. You broke the law deliberately and then tried to cover your tracks. I want you to think about how that looks. Pretty shitty, right?'

Solly speaks up. 'Not to me. Maybe not to a lot of people. What about the man in the street? I say the man in the street understands better than you do.'

'The man in the street doesn't pass sentence. A jury will do that and before you start saying a jury is made up of twelve men in the street you should know that the jury will be very thoroughly instructed as to their duty in law. They'll have the crap scared out of them. My experience of juries is that they do as they're told.'

He glances at his amazing watch and closes Isobel's file. 'Okay. This is how I see it. Isobel is going to plead guilty. It's a simple case. The province is the complainant here and they don't like to lose. So she'll be found guilty. There's no way around that. But it will be up to the judge to sentence her and there's some leeway there. What we need is a tidal wave of public sympathy. We've got to place ourselves very carefully in the public consciousness so the man in the street, as you two say, will storm the building unless Isobel's treated very, very gently.

'First, we've got to find Magnolia and get her back here so you guys are one big happy family all together. The longer she keeps hiding the worse it looks for you.

'We've got plenty of time, maybe even too much. Justice is slow these days. There's such a thing as sympathy fatigue. In the meantime, Isobel has to be the nicest person on this planet. We need people in tears. We need friends and supporters making speeches. We need to jam the fax machine in the prime minister's office. We need noisy women holding placards and babies in front of the courthouse. Are you both clear on this?' He stands to indicate their dismissal.

'And go through your closet very thoroughly. We don't need any more skeletons. There aren't any, right?' he asks Isobel.

'Aren't there any in yours?'

'That's not the point.'

'Sure it is.'

Solly puts his arm around Isobel. 'No skeletons. This woman's a saint. I'm the sinner around here. Ask anybody.'

Chapter Thirteen

The phone rings and there's no one there. Three times it rings in one week.

Isobel sobs into it. 'I had to take you. He would have left without me. I couldn't leave you behind.'

There's no one there.

While Isobel was in hospital, the others were held at the Farm for four days, sustained by casseroles from policemen's wives. In the confusion, no one remembered Ma Ferguson who had grown to depend on a daily visit from some long-haired, ragged, gentle youth and, when finally someone did, she was dead of a stroke, just as the doctor had predicted, of natural causes all right, but linked nonetheless to the Farm, another sad thing, a third death, this time a death without a compensating birth.

They blamed themselves. They had visited her because they were, after all, grateful and nicely brought up. Out of politeness and appreciation, they had brought wild flowers and heavy whole grain bread but what had begun as a courtesy had through repetition become an obligation and they were sure they had killed her with their sudden absence.

Lifegiver strode away into the woods, proclaiming shrilly that the house was haunted.

'Of course,' Isobel said easily. 'You haven't felt it before?' She was amazed that she had once been impressed by this girl and her magic bodily functions, that there had been a conversation between them about foxglove and monkshood. Once she had come to her senses again, dragged there by the shock of birth and death, she realized that she had been a ghost herself for months. She held a baby in each arm and was too sleepy to waste time on foolishness.

Lifegiver took a loud, sobbing breath. 'I can still smell the blood. Can't you feel it? It's in the walls, poisoning us all.'

'You'd better go then. Now.' Isobel didn't want Willow to hear this.

'I didn't do it. It was him who did it. How can you stand to be near him? He pits us against each other. He's toxic.'

'Then so am I.'

Solly stopped working, planning, dreaming. Every day he walked down to the sea and stared at it. He skirted the forest where once burls and straight grains and curious knobs of arbutus had lured him in. He refused go to the market. Elspeth and Booker kept the stall going with Booker's brownies, jams and Sugar's leftover hats. Solly got drunk on borrowed money, roared at people who meant no harm, complained about crumbling chimneys and rotten porches but didn't fix them, scared away the drifters who lived on charity and conversation. The roof leaked in new places and no one bothered to patch it. Isobel ran out of buckets and pans and had to sacrifice the floorboards to dinner.

He couldn't sleep. She became used to the bounce and shift and squeak of the bed as he flipped and floundered for comfort, darkness, silence. When he gave up and got up, she barely rose to awareness; she sighed and stole his warm spot and inhaled his scent from the pillow. Not so long ago, she had felt incomplete except when touching him; now small hands held her always and it was separateness she craved. If he was just sitting, as he did so often now, she would shove a baby or two into his lap. Ash was Isobel's baby, pale and thin and bald with only a promise of transparent hair. Magnolia was round and glowing. He would sit silently and hold them a long time. When Willow was a baby, he had walked the Farm with her, letting her in on his schemes. He had carried her on his shoulders to the market.

'Mrs Allen says they're finally taking down that old apple,' Isobel would say. 'You know, the one you're always bugging her about? She says you can have the wood for the cutting and hauling and one day of picking.'

But the curing of applewood implied a future and, in the end, it was Booker who took the wood and stacked it out of the rain, Isobel and Elspeth who did the picking.

'What's wrong with you?' She knew. Of course, she knew, but she couldn't understand his inertia. The demands on her were small but immediate and continual. The future was the next feed. Her concern was for dry diapers and enough sleep. She watched him when she could. She counted his hours of sleep if only because they were greater than hers.

October came. Wet diapers steamed for days in front of the living-room fire. The babies ate and wailed and slept and Isobel got no sleep and slopped around the house in a button-front flannelette nightie and thick work socks. Willow sat at the kitchen table and worked her crayons down to stubs and wet the bed at night and refused to be in a room where Isobel wasn't.

They holed up. Elspeth soaked beans and boiled rice and noodles. They ate their way through the pantry and cellar; apple chutney, tomato sauce, blackberry jam, rosehip jelly. They unearthed scabby potatoes. They wore soap down to slivers and rationed sheets of toilet paper. Only Willow and Isobel were permitted to drink the milk that was made up half-strength from gritty, chalk-like powder.

They fell into brief profound sleep like exhausted sentries and jerked awake, frightened at having slept at all. They moved stiffly and formally, like courtiers, anxious to please, careful of giving offence. They said after you and think nothing of it and not at all. They talked about nothing.

Isobel was sure that scabs would form and dry and flake off and the Farm would return to what it was. New people would drift in. Seed would be sown. The babies would grow and teach themselves to sleep and Solly would make love to her and begin to have ideas again.

Booker tended the woodpile and the fires, rearranged the drying diapers, read the books that had accumulated in the house: Hesse, Steinbeck, Salinger, Christie, Spock, Heinlein, Atwood, Wodehouse, Mitford, Herring, Spark; read them all day and all night, but slowly, to eke them out, and whispered the words aloud to solemn, observant, wakeful babies.

The sheets on their bed became sour with milk and sweat. Every night Isobel vowed to wash them and every day she forgot. November was no time to dry sheets anyway. She realized it had been Sugar all those months who had washed the sheets while Isobel slumped sullenly over her pregnancy. Sugar at the sink, humming, arms up to dimpled elbows in suds; then rinsing, wringing, hanging the sheets out to dry until they were as stiff as parchment. No clean sheets. No coffee. No tea. No flour. No Sugar.

No Sugar was what she had wanted.

She called Frances collect from Nancy's house and sobbed it out.

'She made do. She never complained. She was always cheerful. She put ribbons in Willow's hair and flowers on the table. She ironed! She told men they were wonderful.'

And Frances: 'Poor girl. Poor little girl. A classic tragedy.' This was Frances's rationale: that Sugar was to be pitied. Only pitiful women cared about appearances, arranged flowers, smoothed things over: sheets and male egos and their own legs. They were nature's victims. And man's.

And Nancy: 'You got your wish. Now live with it.'

And Booker: 'You miss her because she could have been you.'

Isobel did the crash course in mourning, sprinted through the stages. There were too many babies in the house. She had no time for thought, no capacity for it, no sober, brooding analyses, no wishful revisions, no guilty creeping toward acceptance. She soon forgot that she'd wanted Sugar dead. Pregnancy, little kids, they make you stupid.

But she kept an eye on Solly. Solly was dangerous. One dead of night, having scurried down to the slightly warmer living room for Magnolia's feed, she found him standing there with a newspaper torch in his hand. He was holding it up and staring into the flame as if it were talking, its subject complex and requiring rigid attention. Cinders floated down onto the dust-dry old furniture, the scattered books, the splintered wooden floor.

'What are you doing?' she shrieked. 'Solly, you'll start a fire! Solly, do you hear me? The kids are upstairs. Solly, take that thing outside now!'

But he didn't. He held it higher, out of her reach and they watched as two feet of rolled paper burned and collapsed in his hands. She hopped around, her nightie dripping with milk, Magnolia squawking, and ground the ashes into the floor.

'Solly! You're going to set the house on fire!'

He glanced at her as if she was prattling in a language he barely understood, then he turned and walked away. She heard the sound of his slow tread on the stairs, the creak of the bedroom floorboards. She fed Magnolia and tried not to breathe so she could listen for him in case he moved again, in case he struck a match. When she got back to bed he was heavily asleep, sprawled where he had fallen across the bed and she had to curl herself into a corner.

The next morning, she found him packing. He looked up, still white-faced and puffy with shock like someone startled to consciousness. He didn't know how desperately she loved him; she wasn't a woman to soothe, to lie, to flatter, to remember that her man was also her baby. He didn't know she had seen his eyes lift from the ground to the horizon. And now she found him packing, his tools oiled and rolled up in rags on the bed-spread to be layered into a single small backpack, a pack a man like Solly could carry forever without even noticing its weight.

'I have to take off. I can't take it here.' He said it evenly, as a statement of fact. She knew that if she hadn't caught him, he'd simply have left.

She had Ash in her arms. Willow was calling to her from another part of the house, 'MUM!' imperiously, then the rest of it mumbled inaudibly because Mum of course would track her down and find out what the matter was.

'MUM!'

'WHAT?'

A mumble.

'I can't hear you, sweetie. Come upstairs and tell me.' A mother's voice. Everything was normal here.

'You'll be fine,' he said thickly. 'This place is right for you. Booker will stay if you're here.'

'MUM!' An edge of panic to it now. Where *was* Mum?

She thrust Ash at Solly. 'Change him,' she said.

She came back carrying Magnolia and leading Willow by the hand. Willow immediately sat down on the bed and began to unroll a bundle. 'LEAVE IT!' Solly roared. She jumped, went white and began to cry. Her daddy was huge, as big and warm as a bear. He could pick her up with one hand and pop her on his shoulders and give her a ride forever. Her parents were very old and wise and always had been. Now, compared to Daddy, Mum looked little and weak, standing in the doorway with Maggie bawling. Her mummy was white as skeleton bones. Where had her daddy got that voice, that monster's voice, a voice like the big trucks that rumbled down the road in the summer time, a voice like the big tree that fell in the night last winter; her bed had jumped when it fell. The babies were crying but they always cried. Willow was crying too and she hardly ever did any more unless she really had to. Her mummy was too small, her mummy had shrunk. He could knock her over like a tower of building blocks.

But then he saw her and made a quiet sad sound and swept her up and crushed her to him like she did sometimes with her bear and it hurt a bit to breathe, but she didn't mind because he was Daddy again, very strong but in a safe way.

'You'll never get us all in that little tiny backpack,' Isobel said, shouting to be heard over the babies.

He sat down on the bed, still holding Willow and picked up Ash too who was tense and naked and as red as a tomato. Somehow he had acquired a barricade of children. He'd have to knock them down, trample them, in order to escape.

'I thought I was doing a good thing, you know. I thought it would be perfect. I thought we were different.'

And later when one of his women refused to be let go, as the occasional one did, she would blame Isobel for it, call her a manipulative cow, dangle tears on smooth fresh skin, lure him with a satchel and a toothbrush and a change of underwear and he would remember how easy it had once seemed to pack and leave.

Chapter Fourteen

Isobel is washing the poison off nectarines when Auntie Win nicks her peripheral vision. 'Oh, fine!' she yells, thumping the colander down – the nectarines will be bruised. 'Fine. Haunt me if you want to. Go on, get on the fucking bandwagon!' Win walks on and disappears through a wall, just like in the movies.

'This is ridiculous!' Isobel shouts. 'Get a life!' Win always liked a joke. She listens for ghostly laughter, but she hears nothing. Not a real ghost then, just a stray remnant in the memory of the house: Win must have walked through that kitchen door a thousand times; the action has been imprinted there. After Isobel is dead, people will catch sight of her here, bent over the sink.

Win looked great, brisk and whole as she was before her bones started to disintegrate like wet chalk. There was little left of her by the time she died. It made a meal of her. She was nibbled and gnawed at, torn out and gobbled up.

More than twenty years ago, Solly produced Auntie Win like a trick bouquet. She might have guessed. Where another man might keep an insurance policy, a Swiss bank account, a get-away car, Solly kept a woman he could fall back on.

There they stood on the tiny, shiny white front porch, all five of them sticky and stained from their sudden escape. Isobel didn't even bother to look at the house as Solly pulled up to the curb. She opened car doors, extracted children, slammed doors again. The rain had stopped during the day and the garden would have looked superb in the oblique fall light, but she didn't see it. She was coping with the immediate, as people do when overwhelmed by the strange and unexpected. The children needed food and shelter. Here suddenly was a maiden aunt with a small white bungalow who would take them in merely because they were there.

It was Halloween. Solly was thirty. Isobel was twenty-two Willow was three. The babies were babies. Were there chickens? Willow wanted to know. A pond? Did they really mean there was no walking down the road to get letters, that the mailman actually came right up to the front door and pushed them through this slot? She slid her fingers into the slot and started clicking the metal flap. 'Poor little hick,' said Solly, rubbing her hair.

Isobel yanked her hand away. 'Watch your fingers,' she warned. 'they might get caught.' But it was the noise that worried her, the steady, rhythmic, meaningless clack clack clack of the mail flap, a child's noise, a noise that might annoy Auntie Win, their last resort.

They weren't prepared for her not to be home. A spinster aunt is always home, or so they thought. An unmarried woman of nearly sixty has nowhere to be *but* home, home knitting and emitting a faint scent of lavender. Eventually, when there was no answer to their knocking (which they kept up for quite a long time in the belief that she might be deaf), they began to look for a way to break in.

Twenty years later, when even modest houses have alarm systems, it seems shocking that they would presume to break into the house of a woman who hadn't heard from them in years, who probably hadn't heard *of* three-quarters of them – but that was the way they thought in those days: that people were more important than property and that they, the young, were more important than anyone else.

Solly had to break a basement window. Isobel protested, but only after the glass shattered, and then only quietly. She wanted to get the children inside, to feed the babies and put them down, to read to Willow from her favourite book, to dress her in pyjamas, to show her that although her room and her chickens and her farm and her island were gone, the structure of her life persisted. She would still be allowed to eat, to wash, to nestle in Isobel's lap, to sleep. It was certainly worth a window.

Solly picked the shards of glass out of the frame, padded it with his jean jacket and squeezed through. He lifted Willow down and took the babies from Isobel. The basement was completely bare except for the washer and washtub against one wall. 'Not like the cellar at the farm, eh guys?' he said jovially, heading for the stairs with a baby in each arm. Nothing like it. The cellar at the farm was full of trivia and secrets and dark surprises. Willow wouldn't go down there. She used to sit on the top step and wait for Isobel when she took down preserves or washing. 'You still there, Mum?' she'd call out in a little hooting voice, afraid the witches and goblins had snatched her mother away. Isobel used to talk her through it. 'Here go Booker's jeans,' she'd say. Or, 'We still have some of that apple sauce down here, want some?' What she wanted was Isobel, upstairs in the big kitchen near the woodstove where they hatched baby chicks, in a warm bright room that smelled of cookies and garlic and coffee and grass. Where Solly whittled people from kindling sticks and Sugar trimmed hats and Lifegiver dried herbs for tea.

Solly hopped up the stairs, with the babies and Willow in front, and Isobel crept behind, thinking of bulldozers gnawing away at the farmhouse, chewing it up and spitting out the crumbs, making it a memory.

'Oooh, Mummy,' Willow squealed, 'come look.'

It was in the black kitchen that she abandoned the image of the maiden aunt. Auntie Win had only painted the base at that point, so everything, floor, cupboards and ceiling, was flat black. The effect was an absence of depth, or maybe it was all depth. Isobel had to stretch her hands out like a blind woman. She grabbed Willow before she could run off and began to revise her strategy for living with Auntie Win (heirlooms to be moved out of reach, needlepoint to be put away). The shrinking out kindly maiden aunt was replaced by a large, eccentric, antisocial presence who claimed rights and had the wit to protect them.

Solly rushed around the little house. He was a boy with a new bike, a man with a free unlimited ticket. He was beginning. She wanted to hold him down. He used to do this to her.

From the outside, it was a perfectly ordinary house. There were four just like it on the block, modest shingled bungalows that have since been torn down, replaced by eighties mansions, square and shocking pink like fat ladies' bums, or bland nineties updates.

The only thing that distinguished the exterior of Win's house from the others was the yew hedge, high and trimmed as straight and square as a battlement, the only front hedge on the block breaking up a long open ribbon of front lawns. (The hedge is still there but, trimmed at whim by amateurs, it lolls and bulges like a snake alternately starved and overfed.)

The exterior, Auntie Win said later, was her disguise. The front hall helped. It was a cramped little cube cut off by doors from the rest of the house with a conventional mat on the floor and conventional prints on the walls and the usual narrow stair leading straight up to the big bedroom. Get past the hall, though, and she'd been up to things. She told Isobel it had begun with a praying mantis, one small green monster to the left of the living-room fireplace, a pale little praying mantis on a white wall, hardly noticeable. And then she had given it a lupine to sit on, a little more noticeable now, and then the meadow had crept across the north wall. It had spread in spots like weeds on a lawn, dandelions and quamash and campions and tall grasses against a blue sky. She painted a big dark fir in the corner one night and that began the east wall, woods with honeysuckle twining around the door that led to the blameless hall. The east wall was dark with Douglas fir but you could just make out a spangling of dogwood flowers. The baseboard was mossy and ferned. There was a clearing on the south wall, with a bogful of skunk cabbage and reeds and streaking dragonflies.

The room was painted over years, unplanned. Months would go by with nothing added, and then a new leaf would appear, a stalk would snake up, a bud would unfold. 'I figured,' Win told Isobel, 'that if I was going to stare at those walls for the rest of my life, then I might as well look at something.' She never explained the west wall and Isobel never wanted to ask. There are tree ferns on the west wall. There are orchids. There are buttresses of tree trunks that lead up out of view among thick, strangling vines. There are snakes on the west wall and lizards and animals no one can identify. Sober people walk into the west wall. Visiting children run shrieking from the room.

Solly wandered around carrying the babies and whistling through his teeth. 'Well, this will do', he said. 'Look, there's a big room upstairs too. There's plenty of room. And that yard's got to be a quarter acre. Huge for the city. We could expand.' His only assets were himself, his family and a pickup truck with screeching brakes and no shocks at all.

Isobel nursed the babies in the black kitchen while Solly unpacked the truck and Willow ate boiled farm eggs, bread and butter and chunks of Macintosh apple. Isobel put all three to bed in sleeping bags under the dining-room table. Wise children, they closed their eyes and slept.

Solly and Isobel sat at the kitchen table and drank coffee – good, strong expensive coffee, the kind of coffee drunk by a woman who knows her mind.

Solly kept getting up and going to the window and staring at the garage, seeing it already as a studio, with precious piles of hardwood and gleaming tools and a faint haze of sawdust around it. Perhaps he saw the Project, too, although that wouldn't begin until much later, after Win died. He sees things that way; never the present, always the future, a happy, purposeful future. The past is like a mine to Solly. He walks off with the precious metal and leaves behind the slag heap it came out of.

'What if she kicks us out?' Isobel asked. Solly's family had disowned him and her own mother was trying to be famous. Solly was a Whitechapel and could apply for social assistance, but she was a Lamb and wanted by the police.

'She won't. You don't know her. We won't bother her.' He wasn't really there with her in the kitchen. In his mind, he was already out in the garage with a piece of hardwood, chipping away at the parts he didn't like.

'What about the kids? They need to yell and run around and whine and cry. They're kids.'

But he turned and kissed her with insistence just like in the old days. He had come back. Isobel stopped voicing her fears.

When Auntie Win came home, she didn't say they couldn't stay, so they stayed.

'Hey, Winnie,' Solly said when she came in the door.

She didn't scream. She didn't faint. She scowled. She was squarely built, like Solly, with a smoker's lined, yellow face.

'Ingersoll, you idiot, what if I'd had a gun in my handbag?'

'Oh, God, I never thought of that,' Solly said, delighted, 'That would be just like you, too.'

'You always were a stupid boy, Solly. Now, who is this?' she asked, pointing at Isobel.

'This is Isobel. She's with me.'

'Obviously.'

'Also, there are Willow and Ash and Magnolia asleep under the dining room table.'

She peered at the sleeping children and was unmoved by their tender beauty. 'I see.'

Pat says Isobel made Win up. She has to show her photographs. She shows her the self-portrait in the bedroom, that funny, sly picture Win made when the cancer began to spread. Ghastly strands and tendrils are wrapping her up; they've enveloped a hand. One is creeping over her shoulder toward her neck. An ear and one eye have gone completely, but the other eye still looks out of the picture and sums you up and finds you wanting, and the other ear still listens, Isobel believes. A man from the Rellai Gallery comes by every few years and makes them an offer for it. He's just called again. He was more tactful than usual, and he offered more. He even asked about Isobel's work. He talked about a small show. Crime pays, as it turns out.

'*Do* you have a gun in your purse?' Isobel asked Win. 'I mean, it's fine. It's just that Willow might get at it.'

'No, I don't have a gun in my purse, but I'll let you know if I get one. There are poisons in the medicine cabinet, though, and some stuff under the kitchen sink you don't want her into. You'll have to see to it. I won't.'

'I will.'

'I never considered the possibility of children. There's not much food in the house, either. We'll have to get some.'

'Yes, that's fine.'

'We'll figure it out in the morning.'

'Okay.'

'I suppose you're hopelessly in love with Solly.'

'Yes.'

'Well, that's something anyway. I'm going to bed. You two find a place to sleep and we'll work something out in the morning. Solly, you clearly haven't found a conscience since I saw you last. You are probably evil.'

'You're a trouper, Auntie Win. Isobel too. Winnie, about that garage. You're not actually using it, are you?'

Auntie Win snorted and went up to bed.

'I've learned,' she told Isobel later, 'that it's easier to go along with life.'

And very soon it became too late to kick them out. Willow had given names to the creatures on the west wall. Isobel had made Christmas cake. Solly had begun to work in the garage.

Win gave them the big bedroom and moved to the main floor. She walked Isobel around the garden and pointed out a plum tree. 'That'll hold a swing. If we moved the cutting bed, you could get Solly to put a sandbox in the corner.'

It was an intricate garden, full of Indian file paths that delighted Willow and crammed with fans and spires and hummocks of rare and precious plants.

Isobel didn't say no, we couldn't, you've done enough. She examined the plum tree for a good sound limb and she looked at the dahlias and saw a sandbox. But she saw the garden too, the complexity of form and texture, evidence of years of compulsive scheming.

'Why are you letting us do this?' she asked.

Auntie Win swore and began to dig out creeping buttercup. 'It's what you do, isn't it? It's the right thing to do.'

Isobel saw another buttercup and bent down to pull it. 'You don't seem to be the kind of person who cares about the right thing to do. You could kick us out if you wanted to.'

'Don't pull it, you'll leave the roots. You have to dig them up. And where would you go?'

'I don't know.'

'Exactly. Family is family. You don't have to like them, but you do have to put up with them.'

And together they dug up buttercups, which were still opening their enamelled flowers in the grudging winter sun. And Isobel talked about a sandbox and Win talked about planting a groundcover: variegated ivy, she thought, or Labrador violet, or mother-of-thousands, which would look good for a season, until the buttercups regained their strength.

Because they were broke, Solly and Isobel got a job at a corner store, taking early morning or evening shifts in turns and earning just enough to cover groceries and little shoes. Their employers, the Ngs, were Korean immigrants and treated Isobel and Solly with great deference, bowing them in and out of the store, insisting that they take the only chair. Isobel tried to compensate by teaching them English using *Archie* comics and the backs of cereal boxes. The Ngs had no money either, but they weren't going to let that stop them. They had three children who were going to be real Canadians and never have to work in a corner store.

Isobel loved the job. She loved the regulars, the harassed, chaotic ones who could be counted on to run out of staples in the middle of the week, the chocolate and nicotine addicts, the stealthy buyers of *Penthouse*, the fat lady and her potato chip alibis. She loved the small talk, its bland and soothing texture; she loved the diversity of response to the weather, from the sad man who never failed to find something wrong with it to the chirpy woman who even liked sleet.

Solly hated it. He was appalled by the need to make change quickly and to engage in debate about brands of cat food. He was sickened by the swampy smell of the big fridge and refused to take an interest in the weather. He spent his time thinking of a chair, a round, squat thing. It appeared on scraps of paper everywhere.

'What's this about? I thought he was a cabinetmaker,' Win said.

'He was. And a sculptor. I don't know. Something happened to us and he hasn't worked in a long time. Don't ask him. He thinks it's a jinx to talk about a piece before it's done. We're not supposed to notice.'

'Pretentious crap.' Win sniffed.

'No, it really happens. I've seen it. He gets stuck.'

'Isobel, I've taught high school art for a million years and, believe me, it's all crap. If you want to do it, you do it. If you don't, any excuse will do.'

Nevertheless, she played along and pretended not to see the little sketches, not to notice the piles of used cardboard Solly scrounged from the store, not to hear the peculiar, shiver-making crunch that is caused by the sawing of cardboard. The result was *This Side Up*. To this day, when Solly's name is mentioned or an article appears about him, that cardboard armchair is referred to. He should be grateful; it made him famous, but he snaps at journalists who ask about it and they curse him in print by calling him a man who doesn't suffer fools gladly.

He bullied Mrs Ng into displaying a chair in the store and before Mr Ng even noticed it, it sold. Customers rushing in for a paper or a pack of cigarettes noticed and were amused, the kind of customers who might be willing to shell out fifty dollars just to own a bit of parody. He gave the Ngs a twenty percent commission and, pretty soon, Mr Ng had painted a sandwich board that stood outside the store and said, on one side, 'Original Art' and, on the other, 'Come Enjoy Funny Chair'. They couldn't believe he would stop making them just because he got bored. Isobel was thrilled. The crunch of sawn cardboard had found a resonance in her back teeth.

There was the driftwood console and, after that, the *Trunk Bunk*, and he had made his name, his fame but not his fortune. Only Magnolia seemed to have the knack for that. And possibly Mick, who's just told a reporter an interview will cost him two hundred bucks. She'll kill him.

'Do you expect charges to be laid, Mrs Whitechapel?'

'Hey, come on, Izzy, give us a smile.'

'Ms Lamb, I'm so sorry to approach you here but you won't take my calls. Believe me when I say I'm on your side. I just want to tell the story in your own words. Give the public a chance to hear your side of it.'

'Have you heard from her, Ms Lamb?'

'Where is she, do you know?'

'How do you think this will affect her music?'

'Can you give us your response to the rumours of an overdose?'

'I know just how you feel. I'm a mother myself.'

She turns on that one. 'No,' she says. 'You don't.'

Chapter Fifteen

'We have to believe that the things that hurt are good for us. All those scabs and injections. *Il faut suffrir pour être beau.* Our mothers' voices tell us so, and mothers' voices are always true, so for the rest of our lives we think of pain as medicine.'

So Win said.

'What is your pain telling you?' Isobel asked.

'That Mother lied.'

Isobel insisted that she come home to die, over the objections of the doctors and nurses. The system would have kept Win in those days. Hospitals were not expected to be cost-efficient and government parsimony wasn't peddled in the guise of familial duty.

To die at home, to die within the family: this is the best way, they say now. Death is brought home, to be taken like a medicine whose bad taste is proof of its efficacy.

'I know you. You'd haunt me.' Isobel actually said that. She could still be flippant. That was when Win was claiming the morphine was better than whisky. Cheaper too, Isobel would chime in, as if they were living in a situation comedy. That was when Isobel first brought her home and they thought dying was simple and clean, a surgical excision, not a long, messy tearing out, as messy as birth.

Let her have died, she would pray in the morning as she went in to her.

'I didn't die in the night.' Win would say, awake and waiting for the nurse to come. They had begun to think the same thoughts.

Four times a day, a nurse would come to give her the morphine. It was only in the fifth hour that Win was lucid. She'd used up most of the morphine by then; she could think. By the sixth hour, the hour of the injection (and sometimes the nurse was late, they knew the minutes, the seconds of tardiness), the pain had dragged her down again; the pain was a drug too, gnawing raggedly at her reason.

There are four fifth hours in a day. Five and eleven. Five and eleven. Six and noon, six and midnight, Win would chant, and Isobel would chorus five and eleven, five and eleven. 'We'll do it tomorrow morning,' she said the night before.

'Yes,' Win said. 'Morning is best. I won't make a fuss.'

'You can't struggle,' Isobel scolded. 'I'll stop if you struggle.'

'I won't,' she promised.

'You won't remember. We'll have to talk it through again. This is death. You don't know what it's like. You can't come back if you don't like it.'

'It has to be better than dying,' Win whispered.

The nurse was twenty minutes late that night. Win was writhing by the time she turned up.

'Pain management bullshit!' Isobel screamed at her. This is what they boasted, that pain could be managed, controlled, even eliminated. But what they meant of course was that pain need never be suffered if the world were perfect, and if human beings were not tardy, apathetic, careless and overworked.

'I'll be here,' Isobel had said to Win. 'I'll see you in a few hours.' Win looked at her blankly. She had lost her way in the pain again. The pain was everything. Isobel watched the morphine move through her veins, chase down and unwrap each curling tendril of pain, watched her rigid body soften and melt into something close to death.

It was the bad-tempered nurse that night. This one was used to death and dying: it was all she saw. All night long, she drove from house to house and grimly silenced the screaming. She didn't approve of dying at home. A medieval practice, she called it. She didn't approve of Isobel, who was pregnant and had young children in the house and who should have feared death, not invited it to stay. A devotion to the dying was a concern of the middle-aged. Those close enough to it to benefit from its reminder were the only suitable witnesses to death. Death was rot, she said. She asked after the children, looking for symptoms. She accused Isobel of going without sleep. She complained the room was full of smoke and flowers.

'I help her to smoke in her good spells,' Isobel said.

'You shouldn't.'

'Right. It's bad for her health.'

'What about yours? Think about it.' They looked at Win. She was more than asleep. She was barely alive, barely there. What was left of her body hardly made a shape under the covers.

'I know your type,' the night nurse hissed. She could say what she liked. Who would fire her? Who would want her job? 'You think you're such a good girl, so kind, so proper, letting her die here. You're in love with your goodness. Slaving away over your poor dying aunt, aiming for sainthood, aren't you? Oh, the neighbours are so impressed. But what about life? You endanger that baby of yours. You neglect your children just to do the proper thing. She's dying. You should let her go.'

She was right. Isobel scolded the children for behaving like children. She felt guilty and compensated with Sugar Pops and Kraft Dinner. The children flinched at the moans and shrieks. They played outside in the rain. They'd needed new shoes for a month. Maggie had begun to wet the bed. The nurse was right. The baby was Winnie.

Isobel sat up with her that last night. She waited for God to render a judgement, something other than the usual negligence, as she watched Win explore the morphine valley and worried that this was why she was willing to kill her. Win was taking too long, stretching Isobel too thin. They hadn't counted on this in the early heady days when morphine was free whisky. If Isobel had left her in the hospital, she would have grown detached; short daily visits would have sufficed as duty; Win's death would have separated cleanly from her life. Then she wouldn't love her enough to kill her; the parting would have already begun. And she knew already – she knew it well – that it's safest not to act, not to run toward the sound of gunfire.

She had planned to spend the night in reflection so that she could construct a logical platform on which to reconcile or separate love and murder. But she found herself incapable of any rational thought. Images flickered in thematic sequence as they do before sleep: the sweetness of a baby's breath and its sad first souring, a rhubarb recipe she had forgotten, a broken zipper on Ash's jacket, the particular serenity of Solly's face when he held a sleeping child, a novel she had read long before – nothing relevant like *Crime and Punishment*, but an obscure story about a wife who ran away. It disturbed her that she couldn't remember its resolution. Had the wife returned home or started fresh? She got up and wandered around the house, checking the locks and listening to the children sleep. She recalled a single look exchanged between Solly and a girl she could barely remember. One of the girls. She washed her face and brushed her teeth and pulled on a sweater and heavy socks. The baby rolled over and settled its heels against her rib cage.

Win's breath was not the breath of sleep. Every interval was a question posed. This time, surely, her lungs had elected not to expand again; they couldn't do it one more time. Then, shockingly, there was panic, a painful, ragged intake of air, a desperate clutching for a few more seconds of life. Just stop, Isobel thought. It isn't worth it. Why do you breathe when you say you want to die?

At four-thirty Win began the motion not unlike treading water with which she now regularly woke. Limbs bicycling.

'It's the pain,' the nurse had said, 'but don't worry, she doesn't feel it.'

'Why does she move then?'

'She can't feel it, she's unconscious.'

'Why does she swim then?' Isobel had asked. 'How can she

have pain and not feel it? If you don't feel it, it's not pain.'

The nurse shrugged. She wasn't the philosophical type. 'It's involuntary,' she said. 'Like breathing.'

She would be awake soon, and she would expect to die and Isobel had wasted her last night. She hadn't considered crime and punishment or love and death, she had thought of recipes and zippers and pretty pictures. She wasn't the philosophical type either.

'Will you do me this favour?' Win asked at five.

'Yes.' Isobel said. Yes.

Isobel asked about messages, last requests. She held her hand and leaned close. Win smelled only faintly of rot. There was too little left of her to spoil. She was too weak to speak above a whisper. She would die soon even if it was left up to careless, slovenly old God.

'Nothing,' she said. 'It's been good. I've enjoyed it.'

'Don't struggle,' Isobel said. 'You promised.'

She put the pillow over Win's face. She didn't struggle.

It's a long time ago now. Isobel barely remembers it.

Once in a while she's revisited by that clutching fear she felt when she had to remove the pillow. Would Win's face be contorted in the need for that final breath? Would she see there a last-minute change of mind which her weight had revoked?

But Win didn't allow that. Her face was calm, only slightly pinched around the eyes and mouth and nose, a little moue of distaste. She had thought of Isobel at the end. Isobel sat there sobbing and waited for the morning nurse.

And baby Winnie was named for her late great-aunt and was born solemn and watchful and determined to behave properly and now for some reason Win wants to come back.

Chapter Sixteen

'Remember to be there at least fifteen minutes early, and tell me you're not wearing that.' Winnie refers to Isobel's long grey consignment-store tunic and the raw silk skirt Bill sent her from New York one Christmas. The skirt is sea green and grey blue and cut on the bias. It falls like rain.

'It's this or jeans or that black thing I wear to openings.'

Perhaps, in light of recent events, you'd rather cancel, Winnie's home room teacher had written. So discreet, so understanding, so syntactically elegant. *I wouldn't,* Isobel scrawled in return, nearly adding *and don't even think of tormenting Winnie with your circumspect sympathy.* But like so many troublemakers, the teacher means well. Isobel must subdue her not with rudeness but with *froideur* and the New York skirt.

'At least borrow Willow's raincoat,' Winnie pleads. Willow has a navy blue trenchcoat in which she looks spectacular in dark stockings and very high heels.

'I can't wear Willow's raincoat, honey. I'd look like I'm in real estate,' Isobel says, a careless little quip she instantly regrets. Winnie's dearest wish is for her to be in real estate. How can Isobel have forgotten how important it is to look normal and ordinary when life is not?

It's the first parent-teacher night since Winnie won a scholarship to Blenheim House and Isobel knows she must do her best to look and behave like a regular Blenheim House mother. She tells herself she would do it for Winnie; she would wear an Enda B suit if she could afford it. She tells herself that she looks romantic and artistic and that will do.

'Just don't even bother going, then.' Winnie mumbles.

Isobel wants to wrap her arms around the poor little wretch, but Winnie's too old for that kind of comforting, and never sought it even as a small child. Did this chilly self-possession begin at birth? Isobel can't remember. Except for tiny flashes of incident, images her brain has retained for no logical reason, her babies seem to have melded together. She can't remember now which ones had a bad time teething, who hadn't liked rusks, who'd been born early and who late. All those little people pushed out, nursed, taught to smile, changed, soothed to sleep, read to, introduced to solids, shamelessly tricked into sleeping through the night, inoculated, toilet-trained, taught to read, tie shoes and ride two-wheelers; all that effort and now she finds she can't distinguish the memory of one from another. And they suspect this. They demand anecdotal evidence in the form of cute baby stories. They snatch what little bits of her attention they can. Every one of the nine of them must be seen as special, every one condemns her as unfair, each one feels neglected and undervalued in some way.

Isobel pulls up her knee-high stockings. If she can't hug Winnie, she will be on time for the parent-teacher conference. It comes to the same thing.

Monty scurries in like a small hysterical animal and heads straight for the New York skirt. Marnie swoops down just in time, grabs him and carries him howling out of the room.

'I told him to wash his hands,' she shouts over the noise.

They hear her clumping down the hall. 'Monty, if you don't shut up, I'll have to hurt your feelings.'

His frantic pleas reach back, rising in pitch: 'No! No! Pleeeease don't hurt my feelings!'

Isobel sits very still. She could hold Monty until he accomplished calm and in the process get covered in tears and snot. Her outfit, if unconventional, is at least clean. She can so easily make Monty happy, while Winnie's great sadness is beyond her scope. Perhaps this is why she can't remember her children as individual babies: the demands of babies, though immediately vital, are so easily satisfied. Teenagers are harder. What teenagers seem to require of parents is a pablum-like consistency, bland, smooth, inoffensively salutary. Foible and fault are not permitted.

And now, Isobel must go forth and meet the teacher who knows just as anyone does who stands in line at the supermarket that Winnie's parents are bursting with foible and fault. Poor Winnie.

But this teacher, for all her pushy empathy, won't present a serious problem, because Winnie is not a problem child. A serious, hard-working student, a delight to have in the class; these are the evaluative clichés that apply to Winnie, just as Mick must organize his time and Suzannah mustn't socialize in class.

Isobel will be shown Winnie's tidy, logical essays with headings underlined in red and sources alphabetized. She will behave impeccably and sop up the teacher's praise and come home and dribble it over Winnie, and splash it over Solly in Winnie's presence. It's the best she can do. It's too late to be normal.

Even at the public school which the younger kids attend, an institution Isobel knows intimately, often better than its staff, after years and years of taking groups on field trips and supervising skating and running penny drives; even there, where surely she has earned a bit of good will, there is suspicion. Last week, the new principal summoned her for a meeting because Mick had used the library Internet to call up the *Hustler* page.

'We expect our children to understand appropriate behaviour, Mrs Whitechapel,' she remarked with heavy verbal underlinings, as if Isobel had been training her children in delinquency, vandalism and violence in the mistaken belief that these were desirable qualities.

'Of course. I understand. At least it shows he's mastered some computer skills,' Isobel said. The new principal registered dismay but Mick's teacher laughed.

'How's Magnolia? I knew you guys would make the tabloids sooner or later,' she said easily. The principal stiffened. She was prepared to think the worst of Mick's home environment but certainly not to discuss it with his parent.

'Don't even talk about it. Do you think they'll drum me off the lice patrol?'

'How is she?'

'We don't know. We don't even know where she is.'

'She'll survive, you know. She's a survivor. She survived me. She survived Tolmie Elementary. She survived Marlborough Secondary. She'll make it.'

Isobel wasn't so sure. Magnolia was such a lucky and unlucky child. Lucky to be born at all, unlucky to be born out of death. Lucky to be loved, unlucky to belong to the state, lucky to be stolen away, unlucky to be different. Isobel had hoped she'd blend in, become just another of the ever more numerous Whitechapels, a face in the crowd, a book in a library, but she stood out from the beginning. It was easy to infer pointed interest from a chance remark. Behind the bland prattle of kindergarten mothers there might be bureaucrats, private eyes and other official busybodies. Isobel had to invent a sister with precisely that peachy colouring, that round and fleshy build; this sister had to be introduced into casual conversation.

She watched closely for signs of damage in Magnolia, fearing always that she had picked up a little of death at her birth. And perhaps she had. She was different from the start. Symbols, letters and numbers, mystified her. Reading was torture. She'd race past words, jumble them, panting, fists clenched with the effort of it, streak on to finish and be allowed to escape. One squiggle followed by another squiggle simply couldn't have meaning. Dog and god were indistinguishable.

'She could tie her shoes when she was three,' Isobel had said desperately to the grade one teacher.

'If only she would sit still, we'd be able to test her,' the teacher said, equally desperately. Isobel was pregnant. Win was at home, dying. 'Ash is doing very well and Willow was never a problem. The opposite in fact. I've never seen a child so eager to learn.'

'Well, they're all different, aren't they?' Isobel said, hauling out the platitude like a first aid kit.

'So they are. Very different. I guess I'll be seeing that one in a couple of years,' she said, nodding at solid, black-haired Pierre, who was toppling blocks in the corner. She knew Magnolia was trouble. She knew that schools were processing plants and that children who couldn't fit into the machinery jammed it and were spat out and rejected. She mourned for these children even as she sacrificed them to the greater good of all the children who were the right shape.

Different, said Isobel. Difficult, said Solly. Mean, said Willow. Maggie, said Ash. Special, whispered the school. Magnolia was special. 'Special needs' was considered a term less judgmental than *difficult* and much kinder than *delinquent* or *incorrigible*, although the connotative weight of any of them was the same. By the time she was in grade one, Magnolia had a cumbersome tag like a department-store sweater because she was the kind of kid who would always carry one, however delicate and euphemistic, along with the other special ones, with special IQs or special legs or special ears. They said 'common-or-garden' when they meant normal. Normal wasn't done any more either, implying, as it did, its opposite.

'You must tell her not to pull down her pants in class. It's very disruptive.'

'She only does it because it makes the kids laugh. She loves to make people laugh. She doesn't do it at home.' But Isobel knew that home didn't matter, not here. Grade one was only the beginning of the long compromise, learning to sit still, be quiet, listen, make sense of squiggles and do as you're told. Magnolia had to learn to behave in school or she would be lost while still a child, a problem at six, a failure at ten, a dropout at fourteen, lost subtly and by degrees after she had been yanked so dramatically into life.

The school did its best: learning assistance, counselling, each small improvement acclaimed as progress. Gradually,

Magnolia learned to misfit in. 'I'm the bad one,' she would say, offering it like a prize. 'I'm special needs,' she began to say, as if it were a talent.

They tried to find a real talent. They worked their way through piano, ballet, baseball, soccer, art. But all the talents required a sustained effort, and Magnolia couldn't muster that. She had short bursts of intense energy. It turned out she had a genius, but for such a long, gruelling time she was that awful thing, not normal.

And there are more and more not normal kids, maimed by uterine chemical misfirings, relentless neglect, brutal mistreatment or simple bad luck.

All of the street kids are runaways. Marnie's one. Some are the victims of passive abuse; all those lunches not made or provided for, shoes not bought, report cards not signed, comfort not offered, solace not given; a shunning that goes on for years and years and teaches the child that he's only worthy of indifference. Money has nothing to do with it. Some of these kids are less important at home than the job, the club, the fitness regimen. Some are less important than the family car.

Isobel, who has now been run away from twice, is made uneasy by these kids and their fabulous escape acts. She would replace what has been taken from them if only she could identify it.

But, in the meantime, there's sad Winnie and her fancy school to be gently put in its place. There's something wrong with Solly. There's Magnolia, the child she saved, gone missing.

'She's tough,' the teacher had said. 'She'll survive.'

But Isobel demands more than that.

Chapter Seventeen

Sugar was the other kind of blonde. She was small and round-faced and smiling and plump and she looked like she wouldn't hurt a fly.

It was not a period that was kind to plump women: girls aspired to flutter in the breeze, to be borne away by strong winds, their floaty skirts like kites. They picked at seeds and grains like little birds and looked like they could be picked up and tucked under a man's arm and carried away. Every girl wanted to look as pale and frail as Isobel.

They couldn't, of course. Girls too big and fleshy for bird imitations became oxen instead, sturdy and reliable and equal to any task. The skin on the soles of their feet grew thick, the better to anchor them to the earth. They turned terra cotta under the sun and dressed like men, but bled extravagantly and could be had at any time, unlike the little birds who had to be caught and held so carefully.

Sugar was different. Her sweet, dimpled roundness suggested a fruit in perfect ripeness, so ripe it might bruise and spoil when picked but so promising of lush and juicy eating that the risk of its ruin only made it more tempting.

Isobel was cutting up seed potatoes the day Sugar came. Whit came too, of course. Whit's coming was going to matter but, in Isobel's mind, the day was always marked as the day Sugar came.

She knew from the way Solly pulled the truck in, the way he swept it around the driveway, the way he jumped out and walked around to the passenger door, the way Sugar opened the door first and didn't take his hand but jumped down with lifted skirts and laughed in his face.

Sugar turned and looked up at the farmhouse, one hand

clamped on the crown of her straw hat. She looked like she was buying the place, so much so that Isobel began to worry that Ma Ferguson had changed her mind and put the farm up for sale and that this girl in the old velvet dress was one of those stealthily rich hippies who came to the island periodically and bought up properties and opened healing centres, cosmic communes, first-class flophouses and the like, only to be sneered at by the subsistence farmers who were pompous about their poverty.

She studied Whit. *He* didn't look like much. Skinny and long-limbed, handing bags and boxes down to Solly from the flatbed, he had the squinty vulnerable look of a creature unexpectedly exposed to strong light. Not a farmer, not a builder or a craftsman − another lost wanderer − they had more than enough of those. She watched Solly watching Sugar and felt the knife slip in her hand and put it down quickly. She had fallen hopelessly in love with a man who loved women. There had already been women, casual, careless girls to whom sex was a gesture of amity, a physical tic. Solly tired of them and they drifted off and Isobel pretended they'd never been there.

Sugar and Whit came from Alabama and to Isobel their voices contained plantations and mint juleps and entrenched stupidity. Sugar's real name, she told them, was Eunice, but from the time she was just a bit everyone had called her Sugar and now she guessed she was stuck with it. Sugar didn't quite say 'I declare' or 'land sakes' but expressions such as these were inferred by the ear within the long vowels and lazy consonants, the sound of sweaty languor and slow sex.

'I told your man, I said, what will she say? Bringin' two strangers into her home.' Her voice was just a bit too slow, too thick, too full of honey, a deliberate foil to their northern twang as if the accent had intensified through contrast, like Frances's English vowels, which had yearly grown plummier in exile.

Isobel found a brown paper bag and dropped the potatoes into it. 'Solly's always bringing strangers home from the market,' she said. 'Everyone's always welcome. That's the policy.'

Then she smiled and filled the kettle and wiped potato dirt off the kitchen table.

Sugar peered into the bag. 'You got enough eyes here?' she asked. 'You need at least a coupla eyes. Three's best.'

'They're fine,' Isobel said, taking the bag from her and putting it away in the dark. 'You won't meet everyone till dinner. Most of them are in the woods, clearing. You probably saw Elspeth at the road stand. We tried doing it by donation, but it turns out people just don't donate enough, so now one of us has to be there all day. There's our baby, too, but she's still asleep.' She hadn't yet mastered a nonchalant tone of voice when speaking of Willow. She still couldn't say *baby* without it sounding like a boast.

'Well, this place truly has charm. Don't you think so, Whit? I said so on the boat too. This is just the most charming place.'

'I'll show you around. There's plenty of empty rooms upstairs. You can pick whichever one you like.'

She took Sugar through the big dark hall, a dumping ground littered with the passing fancies of people who had long since moved on: boots and coats and shoes and hand tools and seed packages and books and lengths of string and stakes and elastic bands and beach glass and pieces of driftwood and clots of mud dried to powder and straw hats and eagle feathers and walking sticks and socks and blue glass floaters from Japanese fishing nets and pieces of bleached bone that someone hoped to identify. Nobody ever tidied the hall. There was always the possibility that something in it would come in handy, would inspire and, anyway, no one approved of the compulsive purge that had become necessary to clean the place.

The living room had been two rooms divided by pocket doors when the house was new. The front parlour had been a show room, to be used only for grand company; the back parlour was where the family lived. Now the rooms functioned as one, with occupancy shifting from front to back according to the season. There were not enough tables and too many scrounged couches that sighed puffs of antique dust. Books and seed catalogues lay open where they'd last been looked at beside dirty ashtrays on tabletops scarred by casual cigarettes. The mantelpiece was for treasures: rocks and shells, a pencil sketch of Willow asleep in the pram, an old parlour clock without its workings, a fragment of blue-painted gingerbread that Solly had found in the barn, an eggcup full of snowdrops. The maroon velvet curtains were mottled by the sun and held together by habit and grime, they were so old and beautiful no one dared to shake them out for fear they'd fall apart. Nothing was new and nothing was clean and most of the furniture had been found down the side of an embankment, or rather, as Solly preferred to put it, had been selected from down the side of an embankment. Isobel adored it.

'It must be hard to find the time to dust with a baby to care for,' Sugar said, heading for the stairs with an air of purpose. She was right, she was right. It was dusty, too dusty and the coupling within that remark of the words baby and dust struck Isobel a sudden reviving slap. It was too dusty. She must dust.

They chose the big back bedroom that the two boys from Alberta had used. It had a mattress on the floor and hangers in the closet and a table and chair that one of the boys had hauled away from a garage sale because he claimed to be a poet and insisted that he needed quiet to work. In no time at all, Sugar had furnished it with a bed and a dresser that she stripped in the yard and a carved oval mirror and two small pale blue chairs. She found an old lace tablecloth at the thrift shop and hung it over the window and the patchy shifting light made artful comments of the stains on the plaster and the gouges in the floor.

They said they'd come north to a Montreal blizzard and had drifted west in an attempt to outrun the cold. 'Cold! There I was all wrapped up like a big old bear and still I was cold, wasn't I, Whit?' (Sugar maintained that to dodge to Canada had been an error. Southerners, she felt, should dodge south.)

They worked tobacco in the Niagara Peninsula when summer came again and then they tackled the Prairies like a hard assignment. They loved Vancouver until January, but by then Sugar had heard about the islands, which were said to be warm and sunny ('and I guess to you all it might seem that way,' she later conceded, wrapping a shawl around her shoulders and resenting March).

In Vancouver, Sugar had begun to buy straw hats in bulk from Chinatown. She dressed them in dried flowers and ribbons and tiny birds that Whit carved from dried mushrooms, and sold them in stores on Fourth Avenue among patchouli and hookahs and Indian muslin. She never paid more than the best price for ribbon and never accepted less than a hat was worth. Her hard head for business and profound respect for money were concealed, in deference to fashionable thought, under a cover of cushiony charm.

It had been, she said, her lifelong desire to be a nurse, to ease suffering, to bring comfort. After high school, she'd gone to Atlanta to train. *But nursing, why now that's a filthy job, you would just die if you knew what nurses have to do. I can't even speak of it in mixed company.* She'd nursed Whit – they never found out what for – it might have mattered. *Whit's people are quality, you understand, an old Georgia family. They could have bought him out if they'd had a mind to, but they're military from way back, so Whit was obliged to go, and Whit is just a rebel, that's all. And now, wouldn't you just know it, there's talk of ending that old war and my poor Whit's an outlaw. The plain truth is, he'd have been Stateside the whole time. And now here we are,* she would break off and sigh, a woman who had stood by her man. She couldn't see that Whit, a gentle stringbean, would no sooner go to war than slice off his own arm. She didn't care that he could read the sky for storms and divine the soil by holding it in his hand. She was a busy, bustling person and, on the days when Whit sat and stared at the pond, she'd nag about chores or forcefeed him or feel his forehead. Contemplation was not natural to her and she mistrusted it.

She preferred the days when he got up at dawn and sank fence post after fence post without stopping. She'd bring them out to admire the speed of his work; she'd draw their attention to the exact perpendicularity of each post. 'Just look what Whit has done,' she'd say, as Whit moved grimly on. 'Just look.'

Isobel isn't fair to Sugar's memory. She couldn't have hated Sugar from the start. Sugar was pretty and sweet and wonderfully servile. She was willing, even eager, to do the worst jobs in the house: outhouse and oven scrubbing, cupboard clearing, window washing, all the dull chores that everybody despised as bourgeois and could avoid in good conscience. Sugar made pralines and knitted sweaters and swabbed floors. When she felt abused and taken for granted, which was often, she did twice as much work in a brisk and silent fury, a mood that the men didn't notice and the women found convenient to ignore.

Isobel should have been more insistent that Sugar do only her share. She tried at first, but Sugar seemed to covet more than her share, and they couldn't tell her she was wonderful more often than they already did.

If she hadn't made Solly the centre of her existence, if they hadn't become so dependent on Sugar, if it hadn't been a live-and-let-live time, if she hadn't assumed that youth and innocence were inseparable, she'd have seen it coming.

She'd just got back from town when she found them. Solly was almost asleep, sprawled naked on his stomach, head down, arms wrapped around his pillow; that was what really hurt: that in Sugar's presence, having just had her, he meant to fall asleep. Sugar saw Isobel and smiled and covered herself slowly, more out of courtesy than shame, Isobel thought, and told her not to take on. Isobel stood there in the doorway for what seemed like hours. She couldn't move. It took Solly a hell of a long time to realize that she was there at all.

'What are you doing?' she asked stupidly. 'What are you doing? What are you doing? What are you doing?'

'Oh my,' said Sugar, as she dragged a dress over her fat golden body. 'If you're going to have a fit, I'd better get down to that poor child. She'll think something's happened, her momma carrying on like this. Izzy, I don't know what's gotten into you. Have you lost your mind? Now, Solly, don't you worry about me. I'll be just fine. Don't you give me a second's thought. You just attend to Isobel and we'll work it all out.'

Isobel felt paralysed almost to the point of the blood ceasing to flow. She kept saying 'what are you doing?'. She couldn't seem to stop. Finally Sugar took her by the shoulders and led her to the bed and sat her down on it. Willow was yelling by now, and Sugar bustled out to see to her.

'Don't touch her!' Isobel screamed.

'Really, Isobel, anyone would think you were Donna Reed. Times have changed. Haven't you noticed?'

Solly had turned over and pulled up his legs to give her room to sit down and now he began to roll the slowest cigarette in the world. He sprinkled the tobacco in an even line, tamped it down, rolled it firmly but not tightly, licked the paper. It was perfect. He should have framed it. Isobel watched this delicate operation as if it had some meaning.

'Wow, that was pretty primeval. I kind of thought we'd evolved more than that.' He lit the cigarette and offered Isobel a drag.

'If you think I'm sharing your post-fuck smoke, you've really lost it.'

'Come on, Isobel. She doesn't count. You know that.'

'Of course she counts!' she screamed. 'Everybody counts!'

'She doesn't count, I told you!' Now he began to shout. 'She was just around! What do you think, you own me?' Then he stopped and visibly calmed himself, leaned back on the headboard, put the ashtray on his chest and resumed quietly, 'Let's not make a big deal of this, okay?'

'A big deal? What about us? What about Willow? I'm not moving from here till she's gone. She's out. She's right out of here. Right now. I know that much. This is my house. I was here first.'

'Hey, hey, hey.' He raised his hands, palms outward like a speaker requesting quiet from a boisterous crowd. 'That's not what this place is all about. You know that.'

Isobel didn't know that, not then. She believed him when he said Sugar didn't count; she was too young not to believe him. She had leapt off the dock trusting in the clear, deep water below. She hadn't seen the clinging weeds until it was too late.

And she knew that Sugar was as old-fashioned as she was and that Sugar was as soft and comfortable as an eiderdown quilt, that Sugar would never scream at her man (unless he wanted it), that Sugar did dishes and baked cakes and brought cash to the Farm, while Isobel was bony and given to thought and didn't bring in a nickel.

And these were precisely the arguments Solly used when he insisted that Sugar and Whit had to stay. Isobel was free to stay or go. He didn't, he pointed out carefully, own her.

But he did. As she did him.

Free love agreed with Solly, always a promiscuous man, a man who loved women. The smell of them, their light, sweet voices and small soft hands, their weak bodies and pretty, bobbing chests were irresistible to him. Isobel hadn't seen that yet, hadn't wanted to see it. She expected to be Solly's one true love as he was hers.

'I don't want to hurt you,' he said. 'I don't want to hurt anybody. I just want to be free. I'm only twenty-eight years old. I don't need to hear about the fucking pension plan. I want you to be free too. Don't you?'

But Isobel didn't want to sleep with Booker or Whit. Isobel wanted Solly chained to her by custom, guilt and the full force of the law. She took to smoking pot and staring out of the window at the stringy March rain. She became so thin that her vertebrae rubbed holes in her back which scabbed over and opened again at the slightest friction. People at the Farm began to speak in whispers, to walk around her, to defer to her presence, to leave the room quietly when she entered.

She was always cold. She began to shrink, packing her belongings into a single drawer, sitting on half a chair, occupying a narrow margin of their bed. When Solly reached out and pulled her to him, she rolled like a bundle of twigs into his large, enveloping warmth. 'Such bones,' he would mutter, his finger brushing the line of her jaw, his hand circling her neck. 'Such elegant bones.' And briefly she would be warm and she would fall asleep like a child wrapped in a favourite blanket. And quickly she was pregnant again. She could feel the pulse of fresh, warming blood in her body but still she shivered as if with fever. So she waited, just waited, knowing that by doing nothing she would grow round and soft.

Later, she would learn to connive with Solly, to miss the signals, to hang up calmly on tearful, vengeful feminine voices. She would train herself to accept his promiscuity as an irreparable fault, as he accepted each new child, each pregnancy, although he became more afraid with every one – another brush with death, another dear beloved child to fear for, another small hand to hold him close to home.

The Farm had begun to empty of the winter people. The first warm week in March roused them like beasts from hibernation. They sniffed the fecund air, saw the buds on the old daffodils that lined the road, and began to pick up, to look at the horizon, to pack. It was always this way. People holed up over winter and moved on in spring. They wandered off as they had wandered in, disappearing into the distance, the necessary intimacy of winter acknowledged, then shrugged off and left behind like a cheap coat. In fall, a postcard might arrive boastfully from Borneo or Helsinki. Once an envelope came containing a twenty-dollar bill, an anonymous donation. Sometimes the drifters had had enough of life on the road and returned home, got a job, went back to school, began to root themselves; to them the Farm became a nostalgic moment, an episode of light-filled youth that could be pulled out and savoured whenever the bills came due and life was narrow and unpromising.

New wanderers would arrive with summer, but until then there were only Isobel and Solly, Sugar and Whit, Booker, Life-giver and Elspeth. Solly was content. 'This is the perfect number. We don't need freeloaders,' he said. 'Look at us. We're doing great.' And they were.

Sugar had taken over the market stand, and had turned a take-it-or-leave-it jumble of produce and willow ware into a display as coquettish as she was, with eggs and greens and daffodils in salal-lined baskets and a piece of patchwork draped over the back of a chair, a hat flirting its ribbons from an armrest. Sugar insisted that Solly come to the market with her and, on Saturdays, they stood side by side, a good solid country couple selling honest goods. The tourists were impressed.

Sugar smiled and was sweet to poor, confused Whit and continued to bustle, taking on more and more of the work while remaining bland and soft and accommodating, soaking beans and lifting sod, humming a repulsive little tune that no one could identify.

Isobel sulked and did nothing, 'Get happy.' Solly would roar, 'or get out!' while Sugar roamed the back roads in search of second-year willow, nice long pliable wands that Solly could bend into any shape he liked.

'Oh dear,' she would say when Isobel spent another day in bed, or when Willow's hair began to hang over her eyes. 'Oh dear.' She would fetch tea and ribbons. 'Oh dear,' she would say, placing a plump little hand on Solly's chest, slipping another ten dollars into the tin, kissing Whit's sunburned nose.

Isobel began to veer away from sharp implements. She conjured up fatal accidents. She frightened herself. She tried to think of other options, other lives. She too could go home, go back to school, admit to error, become sensible, leave Solly and never see him again. She could drag Willow away from everything she knew, the kittens, the dragonflies, the garter snakes, the daisies, the ease of free time, and put her into the hands of brisk strangers while she, Isobel, worked in some ordinary place, a bank, a restaurant. She could leave Solly. She tried to imagine herself without Solly, but she couldn't.

It was a long sultry spring. The garden grew fat and feeble in the wet heat and succumbed to club root and mildew. Roses turned to mush in bud. The forest floor puffed up fast and spindly and the old-timers shook their heads and feared for August fires. At the farm, they plodded through chores and lived for the daily walk to the beach and the cold, cold water of the strait.

They waded down the road through air as heavy as water. On either side of them, the hayfields were waist-high but still green with growing left to do. Farmers eyed the thick grey sky and shook their heads, disappointed as ever in the weather. The beach was only a mile away from the Farm. Only a mile, they had always said, practically on the property! After they walked the mile that day, they collapsed like marathoners into the cold shallow water on the edge of the ocean. Whit peeled Willow's fat legs off his neck and shoulders and set her on her feet and gave her a bucket and shovel. Willow stood still and took a long hard look at the water. The waves had knocked her off her feet once and now she treated them like shysters. She took their measure and retreated several steps backward and began to scoop out a hollow into which the waves could be imprisoned and subdued and taught to behave themselves. She was an easy, self-absorbed child, who would happily spend an hour washing sticks and shells and arranging them in a complex pattern like a lacy cloth spread out on the flat beach.

Once Willow was settled, Isobel turned and watched the tide edge away. The waves weren't con men at all, but hypnotists.

When Sugar came, cool little snowdrops had been in bloom; now peonies lolled like courtesans against stiff irises in tobacco and indigo blue. The earth was filling up as if bare ground was an affront to its fertility. Although it was only late spring, the fast, flimsy growth made the year seemed old and jaded and about to collapse from exhaustion.

Whit wandered down the beach and Lifegiver, who liked to fry in homage to the sun, stretched out naked. Her broad body looked better bare than clothed. Plaid shirts and jeans did nothing to cover the size of her breasts or the breadth of her bum, but they did nothing to celebrate them either. Now, under the thick hot cloud cover, she seemed to turn brown as Isobel watched, like Solly who never sunbathed but tanned out of habit. She and Willow, born to blister, were filmily protected by long-sleeved muslin dresses and straw hats made by Sugar. She had reminded Isobel about the hats when they left the farmhouse. 'You know you burn even when it's overcast,' she warned. Isobel had nodded and taken the hats. Sugar was right. Sugar was always right. And now she was pregnant too.

Sugar had made the hats, and bought the raisins for Willow's snack, and bought the pail and shovel too. It was becoming difficult to imagine what life before Sugar had been like. She had already taken over two rows in the vegetable garden, and had planted statice and strawflowers and gypsophila and Miss Wilmot's ghost, 'For prickly people,' she said, giggling at the folly of it, 'some people like prickles.' She had bought lumber and nagged at Whit until he built her a little drying shed where she could dry the flowers to trim her hats. She was going to make wreaths too, she said, for Christmas, wouldn't that be pretty? Sugar liked the word pretty and used it frequently although it had fallen out of fashion. Prettiness had given way to validity, naturalness and organic integrity. Beauty was simple if shaped by nature and functional if shaped by man.

Beauty was never pretty, or so they said.

Last week, she had loaded up on change and gone into town and made an amazing *three* long-distance phone calls to a man in New York who might be persuaded to sell Solly's furniture, even if she did call it pretty. In three months, Sugar had become their largest producer of cash. They drank her coffee and wrote on her paper and ran the truck on her gas. They were growing used to it. It was ridiculous, really, even to pretend they were self-sufficient.

Isobel tried to remember what had it been like in the two years before Sugar came. There had been food most of the time, vegetables and bulky starches, the occasional enormous turkey which was roasted, then sliced cold, then stir-fried, then fried with rice and finally disposed of in soup. It had been an amiable, muddled time when good will was all that mattered and something would turn up to cover the hydro bill. And B.C. Hydro was charitable in those days. It didn't rush to cut you off, and after it had done so, it reconnected swiftly and without rancour. She and Booker had busked one afternoon and made five dollars. She had sold a painting once for ten. They sold kindling at a dollar the bundle and conversational French at three dollars an hour. They had been warm and fed and dry before Sugar. Isobel had been happy.

She dug her fingers into the sand that was really powdered shell, oyster and clam and mussel and crab, grey and cream and blue and pink. Whit was trying to teach Willow to skip stones. They'd moved up the beach looking for good flat ones. Lifegiver sat up and pulled on her jeans and shirt and went off in their direction. Isobel could hear her telling Whit that he wasn't doing it right. Even from that distance, Isobel could feel the tug in him, wanting to be the one to teach Willow to skip stones, wanting to teach her a skill that had no purpose at all. But his stones were skipping far too magnificently. She could hear them counting seven, eight, nine as he hurled them far out into the waves.

Lifegiver knelt down beside Willow and tossed a pebble into the barest wet edge of the water. Then she watched Willow pick up a shell, nothing remotely skippable, and give it an overhand heave so the shell made a high feeble loop and landed in the foam. Willow clapped her hands and picked up another shell. Whit had spotted a floating log and was now aiming for that and trying to get Willow to watch but again this was something only a grownup could do, something not to bother about, something like cooking lunch or tying shoes that was simply beyond her. She picked up a handful of sand and tossed it and laughed at the ocean.

Then Whit gave up and let his nice flat stone fall from his hand as he ambled back, head down, examining the wavering line of debris left by the tide. He picked something up and brought it to Isobel – a bit of blue glass. *Milk of Magnesia,* she said, *remember that?* admiring it politely as if he were a child. He sat down beside her and let it drop into the sand where small bits of blue glass were not entirely uncommon.

And she said it. Had she? Maybe it was only that she wanted to say it so badly. There would always be that possibility. Memory replays dreams and wishes as faithfully as experience. Maybe she only wanted to say it or maybe she did say, 'What makes you think you're the father?'

He unfolded himself awkwardly, like a praying mantis, and stood up, crunching on the sand that wasn't quite sand yet, and walked off to try again to show Willow how to skip a rock.

As Willow shows Monty twenty years later, 'Look, you hold it like this between your thumb and this finger, like this, are you paying attention, Mont? And you hold your hand sideways away from you and you spin it fast as you let it go.' So Willow teaches Monty at Locarno Beach (where good flat stones are hard to find) a skill that she learned from Whit even though she was too young to learn it. But in all likelihood this is only what Isobel wishes. It would have been Solly who taught her, at this very beach, much later on, when she was five and capable of learning how to skip a stone. Willow has no memory of Whit and Sugar.

But Whit did walk down the beach to show Willow again, so she must not have asked the question, only wished to. And it wasn't for months that he acted on it, when they were both as ripe and bursting as melons and the house had begun to smell of babies. It wasn't Isobel's fault.

'It's that man's doing.' Nancy always called Solly 'that man', although she too softened when he admired her neck, a ballerina neck, he called it, measuring it with his hands. She softened all right, but she didn't melt. 'This is not a long-term man,' she said. 'Do something.'

But doing something was what Sugar did.

Even Whit must have been surprised when the gun went off and Sugar's head exploded. That is what it looked like to Isobel, that someone had shoved a grenade inside her skull. He would have seen then that the last resort had been reached; it was then that he must have realized his mistake (Isobel remembered hurling the coffee pot at Solly once. It hit his jaw and blood dripped and she still felt the horror of that sudden irretrievable violence. It was something she would never forget.) He must have known then that what had probably been acquired on a morbid whim had the power to destroy the world. He must have heard them running, he might have seen them through Sugar's pretty lace curtain. He had no time to choose life over oblivion and he did what he had to do with the gun and shot himself through the left eye.

Chapter Eighteen

There was a gunshot and then another.

Isobel got up there as quickly as she could. Booker was faster but Booker wasn't eight and a half months pregnant; he could still move without groaning and a great deal of forethought. Isobel's bulk felt freakish and record-breaking, like the giant pumpkins and zucchinis that appeared in the newspaper at harvest time (beside their proud grower, always a man), inedible, immovable, useless mutants remarkable only for their unnatural size. Surely no woman had ever been this large. It was triplets for sure; the doctor was wrong. She seized the handrail and hauled herself up the stairs. This was the most urgent pace she could manage, and only Booker was faster.

The smell of blood oozed down the staircase. It was as alluring as musk, as provocative as baking bread. If there were creatures around who were programmed to seek out the source of that smell, they would come, and soon, just as Isobel and Booker were coming, predators and rescuers together. 'We wanted to help. We did help,' they'd say later to themselves and to each other, defensively. They were rescuers, not predators, but they were still people who knowingly ran toward the blood.

By the time she reached the bedroom, Booker was already kneeling in the gore between the bodies. They were only bodies now; it was clear they no longer contained Sugar and Whit. In this quick and messy death their souls had exploded and vaporized; perhaps a gentler death allowed the soul to linger a while. These were empty vessels, lumps, meat, not people any more.

Booker prodded them with sure, educated fingers. Couldn't he tell they were gone? Sugar's skirt had flown up as the gunshot knocked her back. It made a perfect cancan dancer's arc, covering her chest and part of her head, exposing her legs and groin. Isobel could see the triangle of her panties, pink rosebuds on a white ground, under her huge belly. Blood trickled down a pretty little hand, along a delicately posed index finger and dripped into a puddle on the floor.

As she knelt, Isobel's baby punched and kicked in search of larger accommodation. She massaged the lumps and knobs that occupied her stomach and recalled that absurd list of experiences that were not recommended for pregnant women: shock and stress topped it. Sugar had certainly had a nasty shock. She was forcing back the hideous giggle which rose in her throat when she saw Sugar's stomach lurch.

She couldn't make the words right away. Her mouth worked, but no sound came out. She slapped Booker and pointed and saw his face go slack.

Only she and Sugar knew where the good knife was. It was the only really sharp one they had. They kept it hidden. Otherwise it would be left in the shed or the garden, having been used for pulling nails or cutting string. People at the Farm were always improvising with tools – using scissors to prune, forks to weed, knives to drive screws. Tools disappeared, were found much later bent, mangled and corroded and no longer capable of their designed purpose.

Isobel lumbered back down the hall past the new girl from Etobicoke who had arrived only yesterday and now stood frozen, eyes goggling, with both hands clamped over her mouth, plugging the scream. There was an amazing absence of screaming. Screaming was called for. There was something stealthy in the silence, something dirty in the way that girl covered her mouth. Isobel hesitated – the girl would be faster, but would she move at all? No, she decided, this girl might never move again – so she clumped down the stairs and pushed past Solly who was standing at the open front door, staring at the landscape as if he'd only just noticed it. 'They're dead,' she snapped, dropping the fact like a guillotine blade.

At the kitchen table, Elspeth had snatched up the second-hand copy of *Baby and Child Care* and was reading aloud to Willow in a gabbling treble. The subject was colic.

Willow saw her mother and struggled in Elspeth's grip. 'Mummeeeee!' she pleaded, her voice rising like steam from a kettle.

Isobel sidled past them, plucked the knife out of its hiding place and plunged it in the pot that held the potatoes Sugar had put on to boil. The potatoes were not yet soft. 'I'll be back in a minute, honey,' she said in a nice, normal, maternal lilt, holding the knife high as she squeezed by.

As she grunted back up the stairs, she tore at the front of her dress, spewing buttons like shelled peas. By the time she put the knife in Booker's hands, she had ripped the dress off.

Booker stared at the knife.

'Get it out, Booker!' she shrieked. 'It'll die!'

He used a bloody hand to slide his glasses up his nose. 'I can't,' he said in a conversational tone, as if discussing a small but interesting foible. 'That's why I quit, you know. I can't cut into people. I've tried. I can't do it.'

She lowered herself carefully onto the slippery floor and clutched at his arm. 'She's dead. She's not a person. She's a thing now. A wrecked car. A paper bag. The baby's alive. Please, Book, get the baby out. Please, Book, get it out. You're the only one who knows how.'

'Oh, it's easy enough. Anyone can do it, really,' he said breezily, using the tip of the knife as a pointer. 'Just one little incision does the trick. The mothers don't like a big scar, you see, although in this case it wouldn't matter so much. No, I guess it wouldn't matter much at all.'

Isobel snatched the knife and in the same movement shoved Sugar's body sideways so it slumped to the floor, and made the first slice before she could consider it. It was hard to do, harder than she would have expected. Flesh was not as tender as she thought. It resisted. Force and strength of purpose were required. Sugar's skin wasn't golden any more, but yellow, nearly green. The knife wasn't sharp enough to slice, she had to chop and saw through dead tissue, trying not to think of the squirming thing just below, exposing red and pink flesh, using her wadded dress to sop up the obscuring blood as it welled until taut, writhing muscle was revealed. We're only meat with feelings, she told herself. This is stew meat.

The baby was there, just there, smothering under that hard, red muscle. She thought, even if I cut the baby, I'll still get it out alive, better to be quick than careful. So she sawed and hacked until Booker pushed past her and thrust his fingers into the mess, tearing at it, forcing a hand into Sugar, and, gasping, pulled out a baby head first, a white, limp object, not tense and squawking with outrage as it should have been. A dead thing. Booker wiped roughly at its mouth and nose. Isobel was shocked at the violence of this treatment. He turned it over and spanked it, then pressed the little face to his mouth and puffed. Isobel puffed along with him. Puff, puff, puff, pause. Puff, puff, puff, pause. The baby sucked in its little chest and expelled air in thin protest.

It was to be the most important event she ever witnessed, this retrieval from death. It made her wonder whether death was not, as she had thought, a smooth-sided black and bottomless well, but a precipice with ragged edges to which a lucky few might cling for a few seconds and wait for rescue.

Booker yanked Sugar's afghan off the bed. Sugar had crocheted it all that summer, sweating under its increasing bulk. She'd gone to great lengths to find the right shades of mint green and pale pink, pretty candy colours that were too artificial to be fashionable. She'd insisted on the finest, softest wool. She'd clicked her tongue over mistakes and grimly pulled them out. Solly had roared with laughter and said the baby wouldn't be marking her for effort. Booker folded the afghan in four and wrapped it like a tourniquet around the baby.

Then, amazingly, there was the great joy, the crashing relief that it was safely over that attends even conventional births where the possibility of death is tiny and hidden like a cockroach in the smallest and darkest corner of the room. A baby had survived its birth, whole, intact, unharmed. They knelt in the gore and grinned like fools.

It couldn't last. It never does. Booker handed the pinkening baby to Isobel, picked up the knife and rose, nearly slipping in the muck. 'I'll sterilize this properly before we cut the cord. We should do it as soon as possible. She may bleed through the mother. I really have no idea. This isn't a situation they cover in med school. I'm not a doctor, you know.' He sounded aggrieved.

Isobel hadn't even noticed it was a girl. Her opaque eyes were open. Isobel said, 'Hello, little one,' and put her to her breast. She rooted, took hold and sucked. Isobel closed her eyes and rocked gently and didn't open them again until Booker had tied off the cord and said she could take the baby away.

She found Willow and together they washed and diapered and dressed the baby and put her to sleep in one of the two cribs Solly had made. Willow clung to Isobel wrinkling her nose at the smell. What had happened in the terrible room down the hall was no more or less real than the faded wallpaper roses in her room that turned into fat spiders at night.

'What's in the dark, Mummy?' she often asked.

'Everything that's in the light,' Isobel would always say in a voice like God. 'It's still all the same. You just can't see it, that's all. There's nothing scary in the dark.'

Chapter Nineteen

By afternoon, the police had come, first two in answer to the call, and then two more and by evening more from the main detachment all acting grim and painstaking and looking for someone to blame.

There couldn't be a gun. Guns were not possible among their generation, among people who professed to be pacifists. They hadn't known there was a gun. They had no idea where the gun had come from. A gun! they wailed, a gun! They couldn't believe it. Someone had brought a gun! They were peaceful people; guns were not even to be considered. So they told the RCMP, the very same sweet pimply constables who'd given them rides home from town when there was no money for gas. One of them had bought a little carving from Solly. These were their neighbours. They expected to be believed. But now there had been a gun, the young policemen had acquired hard, official faces and calm, careful voices and eyes full of doubt and suspicion. They felt they had been duped somehow. They had thought they were dealing with harmless, earnest, faintly comic hippies. Now there was a gun, there might be a political agenda, an arsenal, a cunning.

They were rounded up and contained in the living room while the floor of the terrible room upstairs shuddered and shook with the weight of heavy official shoes. All day long there was a scream of sirens as more and more hard-faced men arrived to peer at them and troop upstairs and converse in calm, professional rumbles.

They spoke to them individually, Solly and Isobel and Booker and Elspeth and Lifegiver, the girl from Etobicoke whose name, she squeaked, was Sue, and who demanded to be allowed to call home right this minute, her father was a prominent lawyer, she knew her rights, and Wex, the silent black American who had only been with them since August and who grinned apologetically like a man caught driving the wrong way on a one-way street.

Isobel sat on one end of the couch with Willow in her lap, using her foot to rock the cradle where the baby girl slept off the shock of being born, and listening uneasily to her body, which was beginning to speak of imperatives. She followed Solly with anguished eyes as he paced and smoked and swore and talked and shouted. 'He went crazy. He must have gone crazy! Why would he do it? What was he thinking of? Here, of all places!' He swept his arms out to encompass the Farm.

Eventually, the baby was taken away, detached with a pop from Isobel's nipple by a grim community health nurse too old to give milk, who immediately unswaddled her to look for signs of neglect, abuse, incompetence.

'What will you feed her?' Isobel asked desperately.

'Don't you worry about that. You just worry about your own child,' she said, clearly contemptuous of any mother who didn't put her own child first.

'What do you mean?'

'I mean prolactin, girl. Ever heard of it? This baby's sucking means you're making prolactin, and that's going to start your contractions. Just nature's way of cleaning the uterus after birth. Course, there's nothing natural going on here. Who do you kids think you are?' She bustled off with the baby to the hospital, not taking Isobel with her no matter how imminent her contractions.

By then, the house was full of Mounties. They were courteous inquisitors, calling them *miss* or *sir* without fail, feeding bubble gum and mints to Willow, stroking the cats. Isobel had never watched a police search before and expected a ransack, so the painstaking delicacy with which it was conducted astounded her. She expected stab wounds in the upholstery and drawers upended rather than the cautious, minute dissection that occurred. They found the nail scissors, the onyx pendant she had given up for lost and an unbelievable sum in loose change. They turned mattresses and shook out towels, unpacked the pantry, jiggled books, opened cisterns. What were they looking for, she wondered. What could they find that was worse than the room upstairs?

Isobel's contractions began at dusk. The nurse, for all her prolactin threats, had not communicated her prediction to the police, who treated their timing with grave suspicion. She was allowed to wash her face and hands and feet and to lie down on the couch while they came in small worried groups to have a look at her and discussed with enthusiasm the more horrific deliveries of their wives until her water broke and they believed her and began to panic.

She was allowed to take Willow, but Solly had to stay. The police packed a bag for her. They all had different ideas of what a woman in labour might need, and later, when Isobel opened it, she found two pairs of heavy socks, a mystery novel, a hunk of cheese, a hair-brush, a mickey half full of rye, a waxy old lipstick that had been in the bathroom forever and a roll of toilet paper, but no diapers, no pins, no nighties, no receiving blankets.

They sent her off shoeless and wrapped in a bedspread in a police car with a fast driver and a scared young constable who gave her his poor soft hand to hurt. Ash Lamb was born in the hospital lobby, two weeks early, flexed, red, and screaming for the milk that anyone could have told Isobel was rightfully his.

She fed him while they moved her into a room. They brought Willow a meal on a segmented plate, which she stared at with reverent joy. As they washed and stitched Isobel, people came into the room, looked at her and left. There was a zephyr of gossip in the corridor: who and where and how and why.

'Where's the other baby?' she asked.

'Being taken care of, don't you worry,' the nurse said gently. Willow, full of soft, organized food, had curled up beside Isobel and fallen asleep.

'Then would you please bring her in here, so I can give her a feed?'

'Rest is what you need, my girl,' the nurse said.

'I won't be able to sleep till I see her. What are you feeding her? Please. I had way too much milk the last time. It's not her fault her own mother's dead. Just let me feed her while I'm here. Please.'

'Why should you? She's not your child. She's being given excellent care. Good, clean, wholesome nourishment. We do know how to look after babies, Miss Lamb.'

'But are you holding her?'

The nurse softened. 'You girls. You think you invented love, don't you? Of course we're holding her, my dear. Who wouldn't want to hold her, the poor little mite.'

'Then you know what I mean. Just while I'm here anyway. She had such a bad start. I've got the milk.'

'We'll see,' said the nurse, briskly, efficiently, ambiguously, but not unkindly.

In the end, they conspired, Isobel and the nurses, in the country hospital that held three confused and unloved old people and Willow and Isobel and the two babies and no one else, to enlist the young constable in their stealthy traffic of Baby Girl Doe between the nursery and the Lamb room at four-hourly intervals, furtively in the beginning, but within a day, proudly, defiantly, in the manner of people who break the law deliberately because they know they're right.

'Silly, really. Formula's almost as good,' the head nurse said. Her name was Sharon. She cupped the little girl's fuzzy head and smiled. Magnolia was a beautiful baby, pink and white as newborns usually aren't. Poor little Ash was bruised and battered, squeezed into the world like toothpaste, while Sugar's girl had simply been unwrapped as if from a crumpled parcel labelled fragile and, by a miracle, found to be intact.

Chapter Twenty

'What will happen to her?' Isobel asked Sharon, easy postpartum tears ready to drip and mingle with leaking milk. She felt like an old boat that had only stayed afloat long enough to deliver her passengers to safety.

As hospitals count time, it was day five. Isobel should already have been discharged, but she and Sharon were stalling. For two days, Sharon had left the thermometer on Isobel's bedside table, recalling some procedure that needed her immediate attention. For two days, four times a day, Isobel had held the thermometer under the hot water tap. (It had been too hot the first time, 'You're not a hummingbird!' Sharon had hissed.) For two days, Sharon had recorded a temperature that indicated a mild fever and had written 'possibility of postpartum infection' on the chart. For two days, the doctor had said 'hmmm' and talked about his sailboat. There was good will at the hospital.

For which she was thankful: its rigid routine implied a sovereignty that relieved Isobel of all responsibility beyond the regular production of milk. What mattered was the sitz bath, the selection of a meal, the shift change, the mood of a nurse, the doctor's opinion. It was a place apart. It was not connected to the world where people's heads were blown off. You couldn't blame Willow for wanting to stay forever.

'I knew this would happen,' Sharon said now, snapping sheets. 'I knew it. I knew it. I knew it. You're attached now. We've all lost our minds and now we'll suffer for it. That's what happens when rules are broken. Rules are there for a reason.' Isobel's tea arrived and Sharon scared her into drinking it. Isobel was feeding two, after all, and Sharon wouldn't countenance dehydration in a patient even if she disapproved of its cause.

'How can we suffer?' Isobel asked, laughing at nothing, tears gulped back. Hospital tea came with coffee cream, not milk, and tasted like sweetened sweat.

'Sure, laugh. It's fine for you. You're just the patient. You're supposed to be dumber than a post. You don't have to answer to the doctor.'

'Oh, come on. This whole building is in the palm of your hand and you know it. Who do you think you're kidding? You just let the doctor think he's in charge.'

'The hospital is not the point,' Sharon snorted. 'The hospital I can handle. But now there's the government sniffing around. I've had the Welfare calling twice a day, like they've got nothing better to do with their time than yak on the phone. But they're not going to yak forever. That baby's theirs just as soon as she's fit.'

'Magnolia,' Isobel corrected, as if she'd suddenly remembered a word she'd been trying to recall for days.

Sharon clapped her hands over her ears. 'I'm not listening to that! Don't you dare name her! Don't even think about it! That's not your baby. You have your own baby to worry about. Don't get any crazy ideas. You're just the wet nurse as far as I'm concerned. You're just a silly little hippie girl and I don't know why I listened to you in the first place. All you need is love, hunh!' She detached a dozy baby and began to change it.

'Magnolia,' Isobel said again. 'Maggie for short. Sounds good, I think.'

'Trees! Trees!' Sharon mumbled around pins, 'What are you, a druid? Why not movie stars or hockey players or, hey! grandparents, for Christ's sake?'

But Isobel had settled on names already, and Magnolia was hers. She wouldn't forget Whit and Sugar. She and the children would tend the grave. Wild roses, ocean spray, daffodils, broom, salal, Oregon grape, vanilla leaf, even magnolias in their brief and glamorous season. It was not her concern that Whit and Sugar had families with claims on Magnolia, that her tiny section of the earth, so narrowly girdled in cold salt water, was connected to the rest of the world and that people, no matter how obscure, would eventually be tracked down, that yakking on the phone was not without effect. She forgot that her father hadn't been found only because he hadn't wanted it. She forgot that other people can love.

She nibbled at the skin around her thumbnail. 'What if you went down to the nurses' station and got really involved with your charts or something and when you came back, the four of us were gone?'

Sharon rolled her eyes. 'Right. Brilliant.'

'I'd just have to get to the ferry,' she whined. Whining, like tears, came easily.

'Yup. You and two newborns and a three-year-old. Very inconspicuous. You think there's one single person on this island doesn't know who you are and what happened?'

'Okay, then you take her. You don't have kids. Don't you want kids?'

'I have enough babies to deal with right here at work, thank you. Besides, she's not mine to take. She's not yours to give. She's in the hands of the government now. There are rules, you know. That baby belongs to her family, wherever they are. That's not you.' (Even as she said it, uttered the word family, considered a blood relationship, she saw the softening in Isobel's eyes. Dear God, she thought, these people with their messy lives. Her own life was spotless. She wondered if she should coach Isobel before the police came. Because they were coming. There was only so long a mild temperature would hold them off.)

In the end, they did come and Isobel gave the simplest and most straightforward answers, which only by the elimination of possibility and supposition amounted to lies: 'We know they were Americans, from the south. Alabama or Georgia. I don't think they ever gave us a last name.' Even at that, the detective was furious. Murder-suicides were messy and depressing to deal with and lacked the compensating thrill of mystery. Orphans were always sad, and the thought of an orphaned baby was likely to keep him up at night while the prospect of an international search promised hours of tedious paper work by day.

Isobel looked as stupid and confused as she could. It was surprisingly easy.

The social worker followed. She was dressed in a navy suit and a cream blouse with a bow at the neck. Her expression indicated an attitude as thickly impregnable as a fortress wall; she was someone who expected the worst, as if believing the worst of people was a hard-won achievement.

Isobel and Sharon had prepared a tableau of domestic competence, with flowers in a jug by the bedside and smoke-free air and Willow at the foot of the bed colouring inside the lines in an ironed dress and braids so tight they yanked up her eyebrows. Isobel, who held Ash, wore a keychain ring on her finger, a pink crocheted bedjacket from the hospital lost-and-found and orange lipstick. The effect was very clean and respectable. The social worker regarded it with suspicion.

Isobel offered to take Magnolia home. The social worker clicked her tongue and looked grim.

'This isn't a game, Miss Lamb. You can't foster that child. You'll be lucky to keep your own from what I hear but that's none of my business. We don't always believe in mothers any more, you know,' and she smiled triumphantly as she said it, as if mothers had been pulling the wool over her eyes for years.

After she left, Isobel released Willow's hair and lit a cigarette. She had been right, then, to tell the simple lie.

It turned out that she might really have lost Ash and Willow if not for Sharon and the doctor. They had observed her to be a good mother; they swore to it in writing. (Isobel framed these affidavits. They now hang on her bedroom wall and she often marvels at how brave they were all those years ago, how much easier it would have been to hedge, to qualify, to vacillate.

Twenty years later, there are many shades of motherhood between good and bad, an enormous range of qualification made up of tiny individual acts of virtue, defined by applications of sunscreen, preschool selection, television censorship, availability of junk food, and severity of street-proofing. Smoking, drinking and eating red meat can all chip away at the summit of good motherhood. Love, good intentions and the steady application of common sense are no longer enough.)

Nancy came to visit the next day, bringing a box of Black Magic and the latest issue of *Cosmopolitan*. Isobel wanted daisies, dried apricots and Agatha Christie but only Booker would know that, and neither he nor anyone from the farm, not even Solly, had been allowed to visit.

The nurses huddled in a corner taking the Cosmo Quiz and gently pressing chocolates on one another. Nancy knew them all and their parents and husbands and children and dogs and horses. They opened the circle and let her in, like a coven, Isobel thought, watching them.

'Have you seen him?' she asked. They all listened shamelessly. They all understood about men and children.

Nancy held Ash like a football and shook her head. 'Can't get anywhere near the place. They're all ... what? ... quarantined? I hear they're still trying to find the next of kin. You people just don't seem to have any papers at all, like you dropped out of the sky or something. Steve, Gene's brother, he's been filling me in. It looks like the cops'll have to let everyone go. No incriminating evidence. So it's really the baby that's complicating things. The next of kin part, I mean. Any idea who that might be?'

'I can't tell for sure. We've all tried. She looks like Sugar. I'm calling her Magnolia. What do you think?'

'I think it's dumb, of course. Call her Adele. And especially in front of the police.'

'Sharon says if Solly claimed to be the father so we could keep her, we might lose the other two as well as her. Bad environment or something. Sharon says she'll be fostered out while they try to contact Whit and Sugar's families and that'll take months. I've offered, but they won't even consider it. So, I was thinking …'

The nurses held their dark chocolate breath.

Nancy's head snapped up. She put Ash back in his crib with brisk resolution, like a dieter refusing cheesecake. 'No,' she said. 'No, no, no. Homes for strays is your department. I'm done with diapers. We're saving up for a camper. And you know I just got on part-time at the library.'

'I know that. But that's just reality. We're not talking reality here. On paper you're perfect – respectable, marriage licence and all that, old established island family, two kids, husband nine-to-five. They'd love you. Can't you just see them making check marks all the way down the list? I can see it clear as anything. We're not talking about reality here, it doesn't matter that really a baby's the last thing you need. I figure we could do it like the rocker.'

The nurses were very quiet and still now. They hadn't known there was a plan. They didn't know about the rocker.

'The rocker,' Nancy said.

'Right. Auntie Ethel's old rocker that you hate and that's only in your house when she comes over for coffee.'

Nancy just looked.

'I know it's a big thing.'

'A baby is not a piece of furniture.'

'It's a very big thing,' Sharon spoke up. She'd babysat Nancy. She'd taught her to swim. She'd known Isobel less than a week. Nancy was of the island. Isobel was one of the vagrant ones, who might stay forever but who might melt away the next time it rained.

'There's Gene too, you know.' Nancy said in a discouraging voice.

But Isobel was not discouraged. No had not been said. Objections could be dealt with.

'Yeah. I've been thinking about Gene. He'd have to be in on it. There'd be an interview. You'd have to be awfully nice to Gene.'

'There's the foster care money,' Sharon said softly. 'You know. You mentioned that camper.' She'd taught Gene to swim too.

It became an intrigue. 'It's the Welfare day tomorrow, is it?' Isobel was asked at the Red & White by a woman she didn't even know. Welfare was a stout nurse from Vancouver Island who came in on the ten-thirty ferry. Welfare days saw the crib set up in Nancy's bedroom, the formula in the fridge, the high chair at the table, the diapers in the pail, the pram crowding the front porch, the bum cream in the medicine cabinet. After the first few visits, Nancy had to be firm with the neighbours, who were full of good will and tended to drop by in throngs and tell convoluted lies in carrying voices.

Having made the arrangements, Isobel would scurry home and sit at an attic window from which she could just see Nancy's front yard. She watched the government car pull up, the nurse emerge from it and, a half-hour later, return to the car and drive off. Every Welfare day, she was convinced that the tiny distant figure had carried a bundle out of the house and, once the car had disappeared, she would race across country, stitched with fear, convinced that the families had been found, that the baby she couldn't claim had been rightfully claimed. Wet nurses, after all, had no rights, only functions.

A real estate agent appeared at the farm, an energetic little woman with a grandmotherly figure and the eyes of a marksman.

'It'll go fast, you know. Old land. Subdividable,' she told them as she pounded in the For Sale sign with her very own hammer. Dean in Calgary would do well, then.

The agent barely looked at the old house. The house had no

value; undoubtedly, it would be torn down. Not worth fixing up, she said, what with the carpenter ants working on it all these years, not to mention the dry rot. No insulation, single pane windows, that exhausting kitchen, only one bath. No, it was the land she looked at: the possible views, the sunny building sites, the stands of arbutus, always a selling point, the lichened apple trees, so picturesque and romantic, the value in board feet of timber and beneath it a good water supply, enough for ensuite baths and bidets and dishwashers and hot tubs, enough even for swimming pools.

She grinned at the children and patted Isobel's hand and talked about the past as if it was a burden that was best unloaded and left behind.

She got the building inspector to come over right away and condemn the house. Even then, there were those who might defend the past and seek to preserve it. She knew it was important to act fast and have it declared unsalvageable, a danger. The barn boards would be sold to California, the gingerbread to the junk man, and the volunteer fire brigade would be delighted to practise on the rest.

So they had to go. They might eke out another six months or a year, but already the woods around them were being razed, the portable sawmills whining and buzzing; broom and thistle were smudging the lines in the vegetable garden and a mink had got at the chickens. The Farm was bleaching out like fabric in sunlight, fading every day; soon it would be blank, and then one day it would be something else altogether, a retirement community, a classy resort, a trailer park.

'What about Magnolia? You know if we go, Nancy will give her up. She's not attached to her like we are. She'll end up in an orphanage or a foster home.' Little Magnolia who could only just support her head, who still didn't recognize her own hands and feet. 'She's lost so much already.'

They would do it on Welfare day, just after the nurse's visit. That way, they'd have a week to slip into the crowd. A man whose last name no one had bothered to learn, three Lambs and a Doe.

'You know I'll have to report it,' Nancy said.

'I know. Just wait till morning. We're taking the late ferry.'

'Have you got someplace?'

'Nance, you know I can't tell you that.'

'Well, you can always ... no, I guess not.'

'No. C'mon. Give Maggie a kiss. Tell Sharon ...'

'I know.'

'Okay.'

'I didn't think you'd leave,' Booker said. 'You're not the leaving kind. You're a stayer.'

'Where will you go, Book?'

'I was thinking Africa.'

'Africa! How and with what?' Booker would burn to a crisp in Africa, fall victim to every tropical ailment they had: sunstroke, bilharzia, malaria and God knows what else. Africa!

Elspeth would stay. She'd fallen in love with a contractor's assistant. She planned on babies, chickens, dogs, a few sheep, possibly horses. She'd always liked to see the jams like puréed jewels at the fall fair, the animals all buffed up. She would stay and profess ignorance and innocence and become an island girl.

After all the sad, drifting days, it was like an emergency evacuation, the throwing of things into the back of the truck, a jumble of teddy bears, blankets, shoes, winter coats, crib mattresses, diapers, *Goodnight Moon* and graham crackers. No time to say good-bye, no time to explain or apologize or thank, no time to turn back for one last view, to take a snapshot. It was a run for their lives.

Chapter Twenty-One

'I hope they send you to jail for a million years, you fucking bitch. You stole my history. You fucking bitch, you stole my history. You fucking bitch you stole my history. Youfucking-bitchyoustolemyhistory.'

Useless to argue. Impossible to contradict. What soothing things, after all, can she say about Sugar and Whit? A violent word, fucking, when it's used sparingly, like a chili. Just six feet away, the little ones are eating graham crackers and drinking milk through bendy straws. Isobel keeps her face as smooth as pudding and lets Magnolia scream. I was the rescuer, not the predator, she thinks. I did it all for love. I coped. That's what I do.

And even as Magnolia repeats the terrible mantra, her voice grows stronger and surer: the words acquire a cadence – they almost sound like music, and they get bigger and bigger, not smaller and smaller.

When at last she stops, her anger is not exhausted, but slowed and solidified, a grown-up anger that will be rationalized and nursed along and not easily forgotten.

And, for once, Isobel doesn't do the right thing. She doesn't say *Come home*, doesn't even consider it. There are the other children to consider. They need peace and quiet, ordinary life. If it were just Magnolia, she tells herself, things would be different. But there are the others.

Magnolia might have been happier with that nameless other family in the warm south, a precious only survivor to be petted and spoiled. An only child, not one of many. Maybe this is what she was missing all along.

What would you do for love? The answer is always 'anything'.

'Magnolia, you can't keep hiding. It isn't safe for you to be alone. I understand why you can't come home, but what about

Gram? Gram and Marcel could look after you while you adjust to this.' As she says this, Isobel recognizes in it a round and perfect solution. Frances and Magnolia can prop each other up.

This is so obviously the right ending that she trembles and must put a supporting hand on the kitchen counter.

There's a long silence. Then Magnolia whispers, 'I don't have Gram any more, remember? She's *your* mother. I don't *have* a family. You took them away from me because you always know best.' Isobel thinks she hears a sob before the line goes dead.

As she replaces the receiver, Pierre comes home from school and says, 'Lentil soup? Again?'

And Mick has lost his socials report. And soon it will be Christmas. Solly and Isobel will have to sit down with a pencil and a piece of paper and worry about money. And yesterday the nice policeman with the bitten nails formally charged her with abduction. And they're almost out of dishwasher detergent and Toby's going to need an elf costume by Wednesday.

And Magnolia has grown up and walked away and Ash and Willow too, now she thinks of it. She can count her children now, a finite number that will grow steadily smaller.

They're a strange group: Willow and Marnie and Pat and Winnie; they have nothing but gender in common yet here they sit on Solly and Isobel's old bed, reading hate mail and having hysterics. The mail comes by the kilogram now; the mailman resents it. The flashy lawyer says it must all be read and sorted: Isobel's supporters must be catalogued and contacted and asked to help. The girls eat shortbread and read her mail and giggle and toss it into piles.

(Somewhere in the unsorted pile is a letter from Booker Marek of Médicins sans Frontières. When Winnie reads the letter, she will fail to understand it and toss it in the supportive pile. Booker will be sent a form letter asking him to sign a petition and he'll turn to the Bosnian whose burn he's debriding and mutter *That bitch!*)

The death threat pile is the smallest. The individual letters are usually cut out of newspaper; Isobel is impressed by the effort involved – that someone who doesn't even know her, who lives in Brisbane or Santa Monica or Reading would go to such an effort to wish her dead. Occasionally, they send Hallmark cards: 'Have a nice day! *It will be your last.*'

The letters in the second pile are from women, mostly. These are the touching ones; Isobel can't read them any more. It's clear these writers have been gravely wounded by maternity or the absence of it. They have aborted, abandoned, adopted, relinquished and been denied their children. No one likes to read these letters. They're too confidential, they're like confessions, they're stained with bodily fluids. These are not correspondence but therapy.

Others – more likely to be men – are outraged by her extravagant child-bearing. They say she is indecent, selfish; they find a pathology; the children are symptoms of mother mania.

There's a roughly equal pile of letters sent by people who seem to like Isobel for the colour of her hair, the number of her children, her choice in husbands, her place of residence. These are people she has impressed somehow, strangers again who have made an effort.

'Look at this one, Mum,' Winnie says, 'she says you have her support because she has a T-shirt just like your blue one.'

'Yeah, I just got one from a woman in Fresno who says she's with you because her grandfather came from Vancouver.'

'On the whole, I think the death threat people are the best spellers.' Willow looks up. 'You okay, Mum?'

'Okay.' Not pregnant.

You don't go to Isobel and Solly's on Fridays any more, not unless you're a reporter or a cop. If you're a collector of Solly's work, you jack up the insurance a bit. If you're a student, you settle for dinner on the street. Friday night is just like any other night now. Isobel and Solly go to bed early.

'It turns out I'm not pregnant, just old.'

'You're not pregnant?' He squeezes the breath out of her. 'Thank God. Thank God. I knew you weren't.'

'How could you know? I didn't even know and I should have known. How could you know?'

He pulls her to him. 'Because I know you to be a chaste and loyal wife. And because I had a vasectomy six months ago. Christ, you really had me going for a while there.'

She wrenches herself away and sits up. 'You what? You had a WHAT?'

He groans and sits up too. He had hoped to keep this simple. This is the problem with women: they don't accept the wisdom in simplicity. They refuse to let scabs form, even picking away at old wounds long healed over. They lack the sense to walk away.

He marshals his resources. If she's going to get angry, he'll have to get angrier. Now, there's a good foot of bed between them. 'Just like an ordinary everyday guy who's got enough kids already. Just like every other guy I know, by the way.'

'You had a vasectomy without discussing it with me? How could you do that? How could they even *let* you do that? You can bet if it was me having my tubes tied, they'd have asked for your permission. You can bet on that. Oh, yes.'

'It's still my body. I do have the right.' He makes an effort to be reasonable. He knew she'd react like this, but he hoped she wouldn't. 'Count, Isobel. I want you to count. We have nine kids. Nine.'

'Eight, now.'

'Nine. And I'm fifty-three years old and you're forty-five. It's enough, that's all. Enough babies. You were just going to go on and on and on. It's like a sickness with you. It was time to stop.'

There. He's said the word. He's said sickness.

The doctor had said hormonal fluctuations were perfectly normal in a woman her age.

'So you just let me think I was pregnant this last month? Solly, do you realize I might go to jail? Didn't you hear what the lawyer said? I have to be a sympathetic character, a martyr figure almost. And what's more sympathetic than a pregnant woman? You think menopause is going to make me sympathetic?'

He softens and attempts to take her hand but she snatches herself out of reach.

'I'll make you sympathetic. That's my speciality, right? Listen to me, Iz. It's important. It's time we grew out of this. Christ, I feel a hundred most days. It's irresponsible. We can't even afford the kids we've got.'

'Are you saying we're bad parents?'

'No, I'm saying we're good parents. And good parents don't stretch themselves so thin they snap.'

'I can't believe you didn't tell me you were going to have a vasectomy.'

'I didn't tell you because it wouldn't have made the slightest difference. You'd have made a big deal of it. I'd have gone ahead anyway.'

They sit apart on the old mattress that's long overdue for replacement, where sperm has spilt and tampons leaked and waters broken. They sit awkwardly, resisting the gravitational pull of the trough in the middle.

They sit and think. Solly knows he's done the right thing, that the removal of the addictive substance is essential no matter how painful and risky it is. Isobel thinks about what he's stolen from her: a last baby, an acknowledged last, the last roll of the stomach and poke in the ribs, the last tug at the nipple, the last fat little hands clutching at her knee, the last source of unqualified love, all taken away without the chance to say goodbye.

Outrage rises in her throat like vomit.

'Get out, get out!' she screams.

'Are you saying you want me to go? You want me to leave?'

'Yes.'

'I will, you know.'

'Fine.'

They fall silent. There will be no operatic casting out or

storming off. They're too tired and sensible for that; they're too fond of each other. Isobel falls asleep thinking that tomorrow it will be all right. Solly knows that tomorrow it won't. They sleep eventually, separately, at the cold, canted edges of the bed.

And, of course, when they're truly asleep, they roll together. Gravity takes care of that.

There's tea on the bedside table when Isobel wakes up the next morning, a lukewarm apology in chipped stoneware. She sips it and counts her children. Magnolia is gone forever. Willow's in Yaletown. Ash has moved in with Tara. (He's almost as angry as Maggie. He doesn't want not to be a twin. He refuses to speak to her when he marches into the house to pick up belongings. He does this almost every day. She thinks he will come by again today and stomp around slamming doors, although he's running out of belongings he can rightfully claim.)

Pierre and Winnie will be sound asleep until noon. Mick is at soccer practice. Suzannah will be working through the enormous stack of *Archie* comics she keeps under her bed. She can hear the little ones being deafened downstairs by *Big Comfy Couch*.

Win watches her from the portrait on the wall opposite the bed. Isobel toasts her with tepid tea. You can stay if you like, she says to the picture. Stay if you like. You're welcome. I didn't want you dead. It was you who wanted to die. It was Sugar I wanted dead. But it was Whit who killed her, not me. I only wished. There's nothing wrong with wishing. That's where you're wrong.

In a minute, she'll have to get up and pretend that everything is all right. She knows that the kitchen counters will be clean, the breakfast dishes done, the floor swept, the coffee waiting. For a little while, Solly will attend to these chores. They'll stay out of each other's way, and keep the children between them and when they must speak, they'll be formal and overly courteous. They'll pack the wound with good manners and common sense. Sooner or later, they'll make love. By the time she goes to trial, they'll be themselves again. There will be a casual woman, maybe one of the beautiful television reporters who lurk outside. She knows this. She counts on it. People don't change.

She listens for him as she comes downstairs into the Saturday morning absence of routine. No Marnie, no students, no kids to pack off to school, no shoes to unearth, no notes to write, no disputes to settle. She goes into the kitchen to get coffee and hears him run upstairs to the bedroom. Avoiding him, she stays in the kitchen until she hears him come back down and go out.

She finds Suzannah in the living room.

'Where's Daddy going?' she asks.

'He said he needed smokes.'

'Hunh. I *knew* he couldn't stay quit.' She stands by the window and admires him as he walks away, that slow, sexy, rolling stride, the tranquil authority in the tilt of the head, the strength in the shoulders, the guileless repose in the hands. He strolls down the long front walk toward the reporters and the gated gap in the hedge but he doesn't grow smaller. He stays the same. The distance between them is too short to create that illusion. She watches as he reaches the gate which has hung askew for years and digs a trough in the cement every time it's opened. He walks out and the reporters close in on him like spilled juice. She watches him and smiles. Then Monty starts to yell and she goes down to the basement to find out why.

It turns out that it isn't all that hard to leave. Not when you know what you're doing, and that what you're doing is right. Not when you do it for love. When you go to pack your bag, you realize that you don't need one. You've already got all you need.

When you walk outside to tell the reporters that you're leaving your wife and many children, you're as cool as a clean sheet. When they ask you how you can desert Isobel at such a time, with the trial coming up and all she has to bear, you say it's none of your affair, it was all Isobel's doing. You're an artist; you can't be held responsible. You have to look into the camera. You have to look it straight in the eye and say it like a bastard.

BARBARA WOODLEY

Jane Barker Wright was born in 1953 and educated in Ontario. She lives with her husband in Vancouver. They have a moderate number of children.

Her first novel, The Tasmanian Tiger, was published by Polestar Press in 1988. She has written a book column for Horticulture magazine for many years.